JOIN THE CLUB, MAGGIE DIAZ

Written by **NINA MORENO**
Illustrated by **COURTNEY LOVETT**

SCHOLASTIC INC.

To Lucia,
for being my hilarious sidekick and office
buddy in a very tough year of virtual learning,
way too many deadlines, and terrible Wi-Fi

✸ CHAPTER 1 ✸

For the first time in my life, I can't wait to go back to school.

twelve

pimple that's still deciding what it wants to be

messy, wavy hair

due-for-laundry shirt

clunky watch

unwilling middle child

ready for seventh grade

Bring on the first day of seventh grade!

I'm no longer a lowly sixth grader with no social media presence thanks to my strict mother, who makes me wear a clunky watch meant for toddlers. I can only text her on it. It's ridiculous, but my Very Cuban mother got it for me after I started riding my bike to school so she can always track me through GPS.

Even though I'm still stuck with the embarrassing accessory, Mami says I can get an *actual* phone if my report card is good.

And after my awful summer, I plan to make it *spectacular*. (See? I'm even using vocabulary words now.)

List of Reasons Why Maggie Diaz had a Terrible Summer:

1. Friends were away and busy at camp!

2. Dad had to go out of state for a few months. Ugh, jobs!

3. Abuela moved in and became her ROOMMATE.

Needless to say, I am desperate to get out of my crowded house and hang out with Julian and Zoey again. As soon as I get to school, I park my bike alongside the jumble of others and then race to where my best friends wait before first bell.

"Maggie!" Zoey calls out with a big smile. She has her phone out, playing music.

Zoey

Flutist, currently on a straight-A streak, thinking about becoming a vegetarian, has never said a curse word

Julian

Art geek, new braces, youngest brother with four(!) older ones, is scared of the boba in boba tea...

Julian's smile disappears once I get closer. "You are looking . . . very sweaty today."

It's not even 9:00 a.m. and it's already like a hundred degrees. Welcome to Miami.

"I had to ride my bike very fast or else miss telling you both the big news." I also super missed them. I high-five both of them.

Zoey and Julian are next-door neighbors and have known each other longer, but the three of us became best friends during a group project in fourth grade. It was about ways to help bees and we crushed it.

Super smarts and great presenter

Art and positivity

Willing to get close to bees

Zoey's face scrunches up. "Is your big news that you forgot to take a shower?"

I sniff my shirt. I'm good.

"Drumroll, please," I ask, and Zoey taps rapidly against Julian's backpack. "I'm getting a phone!"

"Finally!" Julian says, because I'm pretty sure I'm the last person in the history of twelve-year-olds to not have one. Not having a phone means I'm practically invisible. No texts, funny videos, or games. No Maggie to be found anywhere.

"When do you get it?" Zoey asks. She inherited her older—but definitely still functional—phone thanks to her sister, who is *much* cooler than my sister, Caro. Zoey's mom is Haitian American and can be just as strict as mine over anything to do with the internet or pushing for too much independence too fast. We tread new ground with them carefully.

Caro
Sixteen, a walking makeup tutorial

"As soon as we get our report cards," I tell them with a big grin.

Their faces fall. I am not known for my grades.

"I'm more mature this year," I hurry to explain. "We're seventh graders now."

We're no longer the babies of the school. I plan on not

only paying attention, but on raising my hand and participating, taking notes in a readable handwriting, and getting way better grades that will prove to my mom how responsible and capable I am now.

And I'll get all the way out of my older sister's shadow.

This year will be the year people at my school stop referring to me as Carolina's baby sister.

It's going to be awesome.

"Who do y'all have for homeroom?" Julian asks.

Zoey and I grab our printed schedules. "Mrs. Delgado," I say.

"I've got Jones," Zoey says.

"Hey, me too." Julian smiles, high-fiving Zoey.

I try to hold on to my smile and new-year positivity despite the disappointment of not getting to be in homeroom with my best friends. But it's fine, because it won't be like summer when they were busy or off at camp. And I'll have a phone soon, so I won't be totally out of the loop anymore. It's probably way better this way, because I'll be so bored that I won't have any choice but to pay attention.

After checking the updated maps that were mailed

along with our schedules, we move with the rest of the crowd toward third hall. Unlike our elementary school, West Memorial Middle is huge.

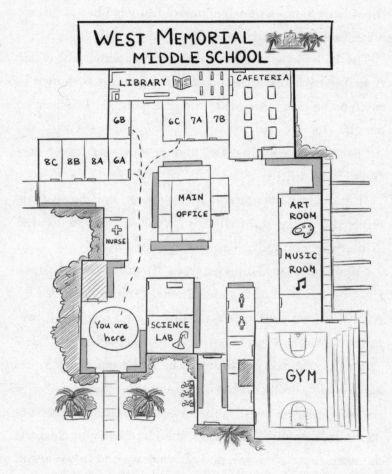

I'm pretty sure it's even bigger than the nearby high school. For some reason, they are always building new elementary schools, and there are a bunch of high schools, including the arts and STEM ones, but there are only, like, three middle schools. It makes no sense, because for three long years, a bunch of us are funneled here until we all get split up again.

The bell rings, and even though I'm excited about our first day back, I'm disappointed I didn't get a chance to catch up on everything they did this summer. I've been so cut off.

"Tell me everything y'all did at camp in thirty seconds," I say quickly.

"Band camp was *terrible*," Zoey says, and I'm a little relieved that she didn't totally love it. "It was *so* hot and disgustingly humid."

"Yeah, mine, too," Julian agrees. "It was at the lake, like, right by the Everglades and the mosquitoes were deadly. Almost as bad as their so-called pizza. I'll just say, I have my doubts as to what they told us was pepperoni."

"Aw," I say, and try to keep the smile out of my voice. My friends weren't off having fun without me!

"We got these awful ham-and-cheese sandwiches that were dry, dry, dry," Zoey says, then laughs. "But then the drumline started a war, and all week we had to be careful or else get cheese slices thrown at us."

"That sounds disgusting," I say, just as Julian laughs, too. "We did that with the pepperoni!"

I don't have cool or funny stories from my summer. Food fights and lethal mosquitoes somehow sound more fun than being stuck at home with a cranky baby brother and sharing my bedroom with my abuela.

Because yes, you heard me right: I live with my abuela. Not just, like, live with her in the same house, which is totally normal. A lot of my friends live with their grandparents. But my abuela moved into my bedroom.

You have a bunk bed, Maggie, my parents reasoned this summer. They decided that having another baby this year and making me a middle child at the age of twelve was a great idea.

My parents are not reasonable people.

The rest of the day is a blur of new classes and teachers. Thankfully, with no homework assigned!

After school, I drop my backpack by the door and start to kick off my shoes.

"Pick that up," Mom calls out from somewhere in the kitchen before I even get my left sneaker off. How did she see me? I glare at my tattletale watch.

"How was your first day?" Mom asks me while she clips coupons at the table. Lucas is strapped to her chest. My six-month-old brother kicks his feet and starts to growl. Last year, I asked my parents for a dog, not a baby brother.

"Amazing!" I say, and Mom cuts me a look of disbelief.

The smoother the bun, the better the mood

Lucas

College student, one semester left until graduation

I reel my smile in a bit. The day was okay. I had que-sadillas for lunch, I picked desks that were in the front row so each of my teachers knows what's up, and I have classes with both Zoey and Julian. I didn't get to crack open any of my brand-new notebooks yet or show off my new big brain outlook since it was only the boring first day get-to-know-each-other stuff.

List of Five Fast Facts about Maggie Diaz:

1. I have two best friends.

2. I am my family's official lizard catcher whenever one slips inside from our yard (which happens a lot, because hello, Miami!).

3. The scars on my knuckles are from the time I tried to ride a skateboard... sitting down.

4. I hate strawberries   but love raspberries.

5. I've never been on an airplane.

The door opens and my sister strolls in, wearing sneakers and running clothes. She calls out hellos and then goes right to the water dispenser in the fridge.

"And how was your day?" I ask her, but she rolls her eyes and points at an earbud before chugging a glass of water.

"My day was great," she announces when she's done, sounding breathless after downing all that water. "Killed it at cross-country, feeling good about my AP classes, and now I'm going to take a shower." She drops a kiss on Lucas's head.

"Don't use all the hot water," I tell her.

"Why?" she asks. "Were you planning to actually wash your hair today?" Instead of a kiss, I get a sharp flick. I scream and she takes off. I rush to run after her.

"¡No corren en la casa!" Abuela shouts after us.

Abuela's really nice, but she can also be really scary.

Abuela

New roommate

Part-time bruja, always knows what we're up to!

Vitamin hoarder

Caro makes it to the bathroom before me and slams the door in my face with a victorious laugh.

"Carolina, please remember that she's twelve, and you're sixteen," Mom calls to Caro from the kitchen, then looks at me. "Will you two ever get along?"

Breathless, I point at the baby tied to her chest. "Just remember, it was your idea to have another one."

Lucas gurgles like an angry goose. Mom scowls at me, and when her eye twitches, I know exactly what she's about to ask me.

"Is your room clean?"

No matter the occasion, it's her go-to reply whenever we annoy her. Or she wants us out of her hair.

I escape to my room, but it's no longer my sanctuary. (Another vocab word from last year.)

Seventh grade is going to change everything for me. It just has to.

CHAPTER 2

"¡Levántate, Magdalena, vas a llegar tarde a la escuela!"

I peek out from beneath my blanket. I am not going to be late for school because I set my new alarm clock. It's all the way across the room on my desk so I have to get out of bed. Because I am responsible now. My abuela simply likes the bragging rights of being the first one to wake up every morning so she can call the rest of us lazy.

I start to roll over, but the blank screen on my clock stops me. I am *sure* I set it, and it definitely had backup batteries.

Abuela ignores me. She is staging a coup on my room.

I throw myself out of the bed and down the ladder. In the

hallway, I push past Caro to beat her to the bathroom this time.

"It's my turn, Maggie!" Caro shouts as I shut the door on her. "Not fair!"

Abuela doesn't sleep in *her* room. Fairness has no place within these walls.

While Caro aggressively rattles the doorknob and Abuela shouts for both of us to stop yelling, I race through all the essentials.

Back out in the hallway, my sister is fuming. "Did you even brush your hair?"

I wince and wave a hand in front of my nose. "You clearly haven't brushed your teeth."

"Nice mustache."

"Nice morning breath."

Mom scoots past us, Lucas strapped to her chest in a bright yellow wrap. "Well, aren't we all having a great morning so far?"

Caro and I do a little shoving dance for dominance before she pushes past me to get inside the bathroom. I follow Mom into the kitchen. She picks up her tiny cup of Cuban coffee and drinks it in one go.

"Mom." I lower my voice. "Abuela unplugged my alarm clock."

"What?"

"My clock," I say again, lowering my voice and looking at where Abuela is listening to the Spanish radio station while buttering slices of toasted Cuban bread. "She unplugged it. And I don't want to point fingers, but I think she might have stolen the batteries."

"I doubt that," Mom says.

"When will her room be ready?"

The tiny house is out in the backyard and is currently just a skeleton of wood and concrete.

"Soon. This is just temporary, Maggie."

This is just temporary is her latest go-to response for everything. But temporary or not, *this* is the worst.

Mom searches the table and its mess of school hand-outs, homework, coupons, and junk mail. "Where is my phone?" she mutters.

It's a perfect segue. I grandly gesture to the fridge.

Mom spares me a quick glance and a smirk. "Love your confidence, and I can't wait to see that placeholder replaced with the real thing."

That's how I feel about my watch. "I was think-ing we could have a conversation about my bike-riding privileges?"

Conversations are a very big deal in my family. Whenever there is a major change, we all sit down and talk it out. Like when Mom and Dad told us Lucas was coming or that Abuelo was really sick.

I hated that conversation.

Soon after, Abuela moved in with us.

But it's time for another major change! A good one this time, because not only am I going to get a phone this year, I'm also going to convince my parents to let me ride my bike to Dolphin Park after school. Lots of kids from my school hang out there and it's right by Julian and Zoey's neighborhood.

My strict Cuban parents need to realize that I'm not a baby anymore.

"Didn't we just have a conversation?" Mom asks, distracted as she bounces a fussy Lucas and opens one of the letters.

"Yes, about getting a phone."

I need to be careful. If I ask for too much too quickly, this will all blow up in my face. But Zoey reasoned that phone and bike privileges would go hand in hand. And she's very responsible.

"Dolphin Park is only like five blocks away. Zoey and Julian hang out there all the time."

Mom resumes her search. "Five blocks is prett~~ ~~ away, Maggie. You also just got your watch."

"A phone does way more than a watch and that's important." I try to not shake my wrist with the offending piece of technology at her.

If it was some cool spy gadget thing, I could understand. But it doesn't hack locks or communicate with the aging superhero who has decided to take me on as an apprentice. It's useless.

"Plus, Caro got her phone when she was twelve."

Mom makes a considering sound. My heart jumps with hope.

It's true that my older sister got hers at my age, but the thing is, my sister has always been *perfect*. Good grades, responsible, polite to old people, star athlete. The total worst!

While I am messy and . . . forgetful.

Mimicking my mother's voice even as *she* searches for *her* phone, I say, "Responsibility leads to independence and growth and it's important that I have a phone in case of an emergency."

Mom stops. Her hand goes to Lucas's head. "What kind of emergency?"

Pivot, Maggie! Pivot!

"The regular, very mild kind of emergency, Mom."

"Wait a minute. Dolphin Park?" she asks, sounding dangerously doubtful now. "You want to go to the *ocean* by yourself?"

Panic worms in. I want a phone so bad. *Everyone* has one! Not just for fun, but for safety reasons—even Zoey's little sister has one, and she's in fourth grade! "This is Miami—we're all right next to the ocean.

I'm only talking a couple extra blocks, and if I have a phone, you'll always be able to reach me."

"I can reach you now." She points at the cursed watch.

"Mami, *please*." I try not to whine.

"No te preocupes," Abuela says coolly. "Yo siempre sé dónde ella está." She raises the saltshaker like it's answer enough.

She says she'll always know when we cross it.

I look at Mom. Her lips twitch, but she says nothing to reason with her mother.

Caro walks into the kitchen in her

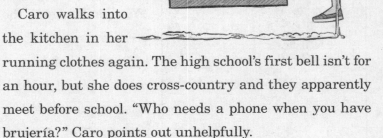

running clothes again. The high school's first bell isn't for an hour, but she does cross-country and they apparently meet before school. "Who needs a phone when you have brujería?" Caro points out unhelpfully.

On days like this, I wish Dad was home instead of away, working offshore doing crane stuff for a salvage company. He would be on my side. Someone has to be.

Responsible Perfect Caro hands Mom her phone. "It was on the bathroom sink."

"Ay dios, I'm losing everything lately."

Is this irony? I need to double-check.

"Good thing Lucas is always tied to you," I joke.

Mom scowls and her eye twitches. I swallow hard. Not the time to be on her bad side. But at least I know if she asks, my room *is* clean. It's the one plus side to sharing space with my tidy abuela.

"Mom, I promise I'll be safe *and* my grades this semester are going to blow your mind."

"I suppose . . . Dolphin Park isn't *too* far."

Caro glances at the clock. "Aren't you late for school, Ms. Report Card?"

I jump out of my chair and grab my backpack.

"I didn't say yes!" Mom insists.

"You will!" I hurry to yank on my shoes by the front door.

"Magdalena!" My poor sleep-deprived mother probably wishes Dad was home, too, especially for backup.

"I can't be late, Mom!"

I race out the door to my bike in the garage and the future promise of freedom.

This time when I reach Zoey and Julian, they're *both* on their phones.

I glance around and notice most people are wearing some kind of headphones or earbuds while they wait for first bell. I have a pair of wired black ones Mom bought

me that I use for my laptop. It's a hand-me-down laptop that I used when I had to do virtual classes. It has a million parental blocks, but at *least* I can play *BioBuild* online with my friends.

But when I get a phone *and* on the family data plan, I'll be able to listen to music all the time, too. I won't be stuck

listening to Mom's boring podcasts, Dad's old emo punk stuff, or Abuela's ancient Cuban songs anymore.

"Hello!" I call out, snapping my fingers in front of Zoey and Julian.

Zoey yanks out her headphones so I can hear the song, and it's the same one she was listening to yesterday. I, of course, don't know it.

Julian points his phone's screen right in my face. "Maggie, look at this next *BioBuild* update!"

It's my favorite online sandbox game. *Everyone* played when we were in fifth grade. We traded usernames and hung out on servers where we had huge battles, treasure hunts, and building competitions. But like a lot of our classmates, Zoey sorta got over it this summer. At least Julian is still super into it. We're working on a new roller coaster for our doomsday amusement park server, the Undead Realm.

"Look at all the new monsters we can add to the park!" I say, leaning in close to Julian's phone.

"Hey!" Zoey complains. "Why don't you show me?"

"Because you never play anymore!"

"Rude," she says with a laugh, and plays the song again.

"Hey, Zoey," someone calls, and we all turn to see Mambo Maya. She's in eighth grade and never talks to us. She became famous after last year's talent show at Fall Festival.

Everyone talked about it for the rest of the year. Zoey was obsessed.

"I love that song!" Maya calls over the music. "See you in band?"

"Yeah!" Zoey returns with a big smile.

"What song is that?" I ask her.

"It's a new mix by DJ Junior Peña." She shrugs like it's whatever, but her eyes are bright. *"Everyone's listening to it."*

"Cool," Julian says.

"Yeah," I agree. The song and Mambo Maya are both *very* cool.

The first bell rings. Zoey turns off her music and I look at my watch.

"You'll get your phone soon, Maggie," Julian assures me, tossing a friendly arm over my shoulders as we head toward third hall.

"Oh, I know," I say. "And when I do, I'll also have bike-riding privileges."

Julian drops his arm, confused. "You always ride your bike."

"Yeah, but I can only bike straight home or within the neighborhood! Soon, I'll be able to go to Dolphin Park with y'all. *Freedom!*"

I won't have to deal with a kleptomaniac abuela or crying baby brother right after school. Or beg Caro for a ride somewhere fun. I won't have to be disappointed when Mom is too busy to take me any-where.

"I can go as long as I don't have band practice that day," Zoey says.

I look at her, confused. "You have band after school now, too?"

She smiles happily. "I'm trying out for jazz band."

Disappointment hits me. Summer is over, but Zoey is *still* busy.

"Who cares about Dolphin Park when we have *BioBuild*?" Julian demands, shaking me.

I roll my eyes and push him away. *BioBuild* is fun, but it's not a way out of my house. Or my room.

The warning bell rings, and I book it to homeroom.

Gave himself the nickname during fourth-grade icebreakers

I jump over Eerie Eddie's backpack and slide into my chair just as the late bell rings.

"Cutting it close, Ms. Diaz." Mrs. Delgado's hand hovers over her threatening stack of yellow tardy slips. My relaxed attitude disappears in an icy cold rush.

She retracts her hand and starts calling attendance. I take a huge gulping breath. New year, new Maggie means absolutely *no* tardies.

✳ CHAPTER 3 ✳

After school, I find Mom drinking another cup of coffee in the kitchen, but without a baby strapped to her chest this time. Her eyes light up when she notices me.

"Maggie! I'm so glad you're home."

I drop into a chair and sniff, but smell nothing. Dinner should be cooking, but there's no garlic or sofrito sizzling in the air.

"I have to run to campus," Mom tells me. "I really need the extra credit for attending this workshop about new tax codes."

I pretend to fall asleep.

She digs into her big messy bag, switching out all the baby junk for her college stuff. "And I didn't get to go to the grocery store," she continues as books and notebooks replace diapers and wipes, ignoring my performance. "I swear, trying to graduate this term is going to kill me."

Mom put college on hold when she had Caro. She must have figured it would only be for a little while (*temporary* = her magic word), but then I came along. After that it felt like everyone was waiting for me to grow up so Mom could go back to college and finally graduate.

But then my baby brother happened and all of us got pushed back to the start.

Except, not everybody. Because instead of waiting for him to grow up, too, Mom is powering through to graduate with her accounting degree this time. After Abuelo died earlier this year, Mom said life was too short to wait. Plus, with Abuela living here and Caro being able to drive, things were easier.

I was the only one who seemed to take a giant leap backward this year.

"Where's Abuela?" I ask.

"Aquí," Abuela announces, carrying an already whining Lucas, and even from here I can smell the agua de violetas perfume she's bathed him in.

Abuela is wearing one of her louder blouses, all silky and bright with *way* too many flowers. "Vamos a la tienda porque tu madre se le olvidó."

"¡Ay, Mami, ya!" Mom says, sounding as frustrated as I feel. To me she lowers her voice and says, "I didn't forget to go to the store, it's just been a bit of a day. So she's going to pick up a few things for me."

"What does that have to do with me?" Abuela isn't *that* old. She goes out on her own all the time.

"Because she's also taking Lucas, and that's a lot to handle with the stroller and everything," she says. "You can be an extra set of hands."

"What about Caro? I'm supposed to play *BioBuild* with Julian."

"She's tutoring today. And you can play your game later."

I suddenly wish I was in a club, too. That way I would have something important to do after school instead of being forced to run errands with my abuela, which always takes *forever*.

At every place, she has to stop y saludar everyone and their prima. And the guava and cheese pastelitos at the bakery never last long enough to make up for how long it takes Abuela to get all her chisme and *finally* say goodbye.

Also, for some reason, she never turns the AC on in her car.

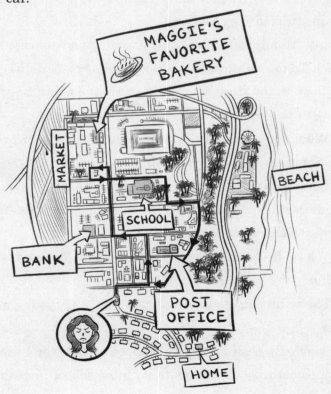

"These next couple of weeks are going to be a little cha-otic until your dad gets back."

"This is temporary," I say, deadpan.

She gives me a happy, smacking kiss on the forehead. "You've shown me how responsible you've become, and I'm so proud of you. I just need a little help right now."

With her hands still squeezing my cheeks, I nod. She has so much to do every day, and it does feel good to make some-thing easier for her.

Responsible Maggie Diaz. Maybe I *can* do this.

"And listen, I was thinking about it, and if your report card is as great as you say it'll be—"

Excitement strikes like a lightning bolt. "I'll get a phone *and* get to go to Dolphin Park?"

Mom smiles and kisses my forehead again. It seals the promise.

"And I can have unlimited data?"

Mom scowls. "Don't push it."

Responsible Maggie Diaz! On the phone plan!

By the time we reach the market, I am in desperate need of sugar and silence. There is no way it's going to be quiet thanks to this crowd, but at least there are pastelitos.

"It's been a long afternoon," I tell Pablo after a gusty sigh.

"Seventh grade as brutal as I remember?"

"Yeah, but if I keep my grades up, I'll finally get a phone."

"Aw, that's great, Maggie!" he says.

I like Pablo. His hair is bright blue, and he wears eyeliner that a lot of the viejitos give him grief over, in the same way they tease everyone about something. His family runs the market and he says he's worked behind this very window since he was my age.

Whenever I ask him how long ago that was, he always says, *too long*.

Everyone in the neighborhood expects their usual pastelitos and croquetas with their coffee from him, but I know that Pablo loves to experiment. He likes to use all those familiar flavors to bake different stuff. I'm one of his official taste testers while he saves up for culinary school.

"These look *very* fancy, Pablo."

He laughs. "You don't have to sound so worried about that."

I bite into one. My eyes widen as rich caramel and creamy cheesecake hit my tongue. "This is *so* good!" I announce, my mouth still full.

Pablo dramatically swipes a hand across his forehead in relief.

My new art teacher, Ms. Pérez, steps up to the window. "Hey, Maggie. What you got there?"

"Best yet," I tell Pablo once I swallow, then look at Ms. Pérez. "These are on the secret menu. You have to know people."

She grins. "Is that right? Well, maybe you can introduce me to your people in the name of friendship and desserts."

Before I can do the honors, Abuela rushes over, looking frazzled. The stroller is now loaded down with bags. Somewhere in the mess of them, Lucas is wailing. She gestures to him like all that noise is my fault.

I sigh before lifting him into my arms. He settles down after a few seconds.

"Ay, pero, este niño," Abuela complains, trying her best to sound bothered, but she's already melting over his puckered lips. She leans forward to kiss him all over his face, then hisses in pain before pressing a hand against her lower back. She leans against the window and glances at Pablo. "Dame un cafecito, mijo."

"Ms. Pérez, this is my abuela," I say. "And my baby brother, Lucas."

"How are you liking West Memorial?" I ask Ms. Pérez.

"Great so far! I get to start an after-school art club."

Another club! I hit seventh grade and suddenly they're everywhere.

"You're—you're new?" Pablo asks her.

"Yeah, just moved here from Atlanta." She smiles and I try not to laugh as Pablo nearly swoons. "This is such a great neighborhood. I'm actually on my way to check out some of the murals around here."

"Oh yeah? I could show you around," Pablo tells her happily. "I know of some awesome ones that just went up."

"That would be great!"

Abuela calls out, "¡Bueno, besos!" to everyone as farewell, and it's my signal that we are *finally* done.

✺ CHAPTER 4 ✺

My alarm wakes me the next morning. The batteries are *mysteriously* back. The first thing I notice is the mechanical sound of Abuela's humidifier chugging along like an angry, dying robot. The second thing is that my room is starting to smell different. Like Abuela's face powder that makes me sneeze and her minty medicine.

It's starting to smell like old people!

Out in the hall, I stop at Caro's bedroom door. She's pacing in her room, her hands and lips moving, but I can't hear what she's saying because of the song she's loudly listening to. I lean into the doorway. "Did you run out of other people to annoy?"

She slams the door in my face and turns her music up even louder.

"Rude!" I call through the door.

"¡Oye!" Abuela shouts all the way from the kitchen. "¡Señoritas no gritan en esta casa!"

"Are you kidding me?" I grumble under my breath, and go to brush my teeth.

On my way to the kitchen, I can make out the song Caro is blasting in her room. It's on repeat. It's also the same one Zoey was listening to yesterday. Middle school playlists *and* Miami radio stations? Wow, that song really is everywhere. Wait . . .

At school, I'm thrilled to see that Julian and Zoey are already at our usual spot. Zoey has her phone out and is playing that song again. A perfect intro! "I have the best idea!"

Her parents don't let her wear makeup yet, so she waits until she gets to school to apply the lip gloss and highlighter she secretly keeps in her backpack.

Julian holds up a mirror for her. "What is it?"

Zoey frowns. "You can't have my phone, Maggie."

"I mean that song! Everyone is listening to it. Even my sister, which means high school kids are, too."

"I heard the DJ is local," Zoey says.

"Really?" Julian asks.

"We can go to Dolphin Park, make up a dance, and post it online with Zoey's phone. Maybe it'll go viral or something." Best of all, it's something brand-new and fun that we can all do together.

MAGGIE'S
BRILLIANT IDEA

"I don't know . . ." Zoey hesitates.

"It'll be fun and you can show it to Maya. Or, like, who-ever else."

Because Zoey has cool friends who do cool things. Including me.

"I'm pretty sure our parents would kill us if we went viral for some dance," Zoey points out.

"And I don't dance, Maggie," Julian says. "And neither do you."

"It wouldn't have to be a complicated one."

"And anyway, I can't go to the park today," Zoey says. "I've got tryouts for jazz band."

"You like jazz?" Julian asks, making himself laugh.

I've listened to her practice, and even with my non-musical ear, I know she's great. She's totally going to get in. And then she'll be even busier.

I look at Julian. "What about you?"

"I'm signing up for art club," he says.

A collection of colored pencils sticks out from his shirt pocket. He's been working on his comic since the summer. It's about the legendary Skunk Ape of Florida, who turns into a post-apocalyptic robot after the sea levels rise and wipe out Miami.

"They've got loads of supplies and this week

we start work on contour line drawing using a grid," he explains with a happy laugh.

"What does that mean?" Zoey asks.

"I don't know!" Julian is delighted by the prospect of learning something new.

The idea of not having an obvious talent like theirs makes me feel lost. I *don't* have one. And I've never felt so different from my friends.

"Well, have fun doing cool stuff with your new friends,"

I try to say like a joke, but I know I sound grumpy.

Zoey rolls her eyes. "We might be too busy to dance at the park, but we're never too busy for *you*." She shakes me a little and offers me one of her *Everything's fine, just be cool, Maggie* smiles.

"Plus, I didn't even get a chance to tell you my huge news!" Julian says.

"Commander Bunny is planning a stream to visit their fans' different servers! We can enter our amusement park of doom!"

I almost scream, I'm so excited. One bright spot in my summer was watching their streams on my laptop. I would

flip out to see our server in one. Commander Bunny is a Dominican American gamer who loves a lot of slice-of-life RPGs and is one of the coolest people I know who still plays *BioBuild*.

"But are you sure you'll have time with art club and everything?" I try to not sound like too much of a baby.

"Duh," he says like it's obvious.

Zoey rolls her eyes at me again. "This is what seventh grade is all about, figuring out all the stuff we're into."

As the warning bell rings, she and Julian start to leave. Together. As I watch them go, I realize it isn't just them—everyone's on some kind of team or in a club. The hallway is littered with club sign-up posters. Some kids are even wearing matching team shirts as they rush to homeroom.

I can't afford to be late.

I'm going to do so great this year! I keep telling everyone, but I have no phone, I'm sharing my bedroom, Dad is hundreds of miles away, and now my friends are too busy for me.

I need something to look forward to and be as excited about as Zoey is about band and Julian is about his comic and art club. I need something that isn't just me going back home to babysit or hang out with my abuela in a room that doesn't even feel like mine anymore.

I need a club. That's got to be step one.

I jump over Eerie Eddie's backpack that's always in the way and stumble into my chair. I look up to see Mrs. Delgado watching me, her hand on that awful yellow pad. The morning announcements start on the TV.

"It's becoming a habit, Ms. Diaz," she warns.

I really need to figure things out before tardiness becomes my thing.

✷ CHAPTER 5 ✷

Zoey's words continue to turn over in my head all day.

This is what seventh grade is all about. Everyone is on some kind of team or in a group.

I thought it was going to be about independence and getting to do more with my friends out of the house. But they're *already* doing stuff, and they're doing it without me.

After school, as I ride my bike—straight home, no Dolphin Park yet—I try to figure out what could be my thing. I don't play an instrument and I can't draw anything more than the loopy flowers I sketch on worksheets whenever I get distracted.

It's not that I don't have hobbies or interests. I have plenty.

But none of those amount to *something*. Or even a club.

At home, I find Abuela in the kitchen with the smell of garlic and onions sizzling in the air. I take a big, greedy inhale. "What's for dinner?"

"Fricasé de pollo," she says. "Necesito que vayas al vecino por un aguacate."

I'm so distracted by the smell of food it takes me a minute to realize what she just asked me.

"What? No!" I hate when Abuela asks me to *steal* avocados from our neighbor's tree. It's undignified. It's criminal.

WANTED

MAGGIE DIAZ

Avocado Stealer

"Ay, Maggie, por favor."

"Abuela—"

"La Señora García dijo que está bien," she says as she stirs the chicken stew.

I look at Abuela. "Are you *sure* she said that? Because last time, she yelled out her window at me and almost gave me a heart attack."

Probably also a bruja!

Wind chimes

Strange plants

Abuela rolls her eyes like I'm the ridiculous one when she's peer-pressuring her own grandchild to jump over our back fence for an avocado. I bet there was a bin full of them at the store, too. But I guess why buy them when there's a fruit tree right outside?

"Because it's not ours," I grumble as I climb, then hop over, the chain-link fence. I slowly walk over to the tree, keeping an eye on the back door and window. According to Abuela, Mrs. García is fine with this. But I have my doubts about Abuela's honesty.

I stop at the sight of a rooster ahead of me.

"Shh," I whisper. "I mean no harm. I mean, not to you. I had nothing to do with the dinner my abuela is making, I swear."

The rooster ignores me. I'm in the clear. I grab a fallen avocado off the grass and turn to go back home.

"¡Niña!"

I freeze with a guilty yelp.

"¿Qué haces?" Mrs. García stands on her back porch.

I raise the avocado up and away from me like it might explode as I shout, "My abuela said you told her it was okay!"

Mrs. García doesn't say anything for a very long and distressing moment. Her ominously clicking and clacking wind chimes are the only sound between us. As I start to panic over whose bones I'm currently listening to dance in the warm breeze, she laughs and sweeps her robe around before disappearing inside.

I run home. I need an after-school activity before I fall into a life of stealing fruit from neighbors. Or even worse, make a bruja mad.

Dinnertime means pushing aside all the junk mail and coupon clippings so we can sit together at the table.

Lucas's high chair is parked where Dad usually sits. It will definitely be cramped once my dad returns home.

I really need to ask Mom for some help, but I don't want to lose the headway I've made with her. She has finally stopped looking at me like a baby and considers me kind of responsible now. But Dad and her always say to never be afraid to ask for help.

I spoon the fricasé de pollo and white rice into my mouth. Next, a bite of the avocado Abuela has sliced and dressed with vinegar and salt.

It's delicious and one of my favorite dinner combinations. For the moment, Abuela is forgiven for the avocado scandal. She smirks at me like she knows it.

The only person not smiling at our table is Caro.

Maybe her junior year has started out as stressful and confusing as mine has.

I glance at Mom. She's watching Caro closely, too.

"How was your day, Carolina?" Mom asks.

Beside me, Caro jumps like a spooked cat. What is with her?

Messier hair

Phone nowhere to be seen

?

Untouched plate

"Good," Caro replies. "Classes are chill, and I got an A on my algebra quiz. And, uh, tutoring club has been cool."

My sister is only a few years older than me but is already doing all sorts of clubs to impress future colleges. Am I supposed to be thinking about that? Are Zoey and Julian? The pressure to find a skill or club suddenly feels really stressful.

But I don't want to pick a club that just feels like *more* school. That's torture!

Caro is still talking. "And Alex is helping the tutoring club expand to other schools."

"Right," Mom says. "I've heard you mention Alex quite a few times since the summer."

Abuela's eyes are bright. "¿Tienes un novio, Carolina?"

"No, I don't have a boyfriend," Caro hurries to say. "Alex is a girl."

"Alejandra?" Abuela assumes.

"Alex is the friend you've been telling me about?" Mom asks. "The one you've been spending a lot of time with?"

Caro nods. "Yeah, she's a good . . . friend."

"That's great, sweetie," Mom says. "About tutoring. And Alex."

A long moment passes where they just stare at each other with wide, googly eyes.

"I really like—" Caro looks at me, then Abuela. "Tutoring club."

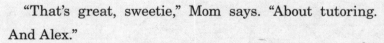

Mom looks unexpectedly emotional all of a sudden. "I think it's great that you're happy and you should feel . . . free to explore all of your interests."

"Explore?" I ask.

"Yes, explore all the facets of yourself," Mom says, still looking at Caro. "It's really important when you're young."

"You're not that old, Mom," Caro says, and Mom laughs.

"Did you meet Alex in tutoring club?" I ask.

"Yeah, she's super smart and does a lot of cool stuff. She volunteers with a bunch of clubs and is on the soccer team, too."

Maybe I could join a sport?

"I love you and I'm so proud of you," Mom says to Caro, and I have no idea why they are getting so emotional about this. Mom loves school, but it makes no sense for her to be so worked up about tutoring.

"¿Qué pasó?" Abuela asks, sounding as bewildered as me.

"Nada, Mami," Mom says.

My sister has a new friend, which makes me think of Zoey and Julian hanging out with new people this year, too.

Between the coup on my room and my friends' busy schedules, I can't help but feel like my plans for a super-awesome school year are already falling apart.

I need something, too. Something new and *mine*.

When I was in first grade, I decided I had to become a Girl Scout. Alyssa Winters was one and she had shown off her killer badges during show-and-tell. *I* wanted cool badges that proved I was good at stuff! But after six months, I ended up hating having to wear another uniform and begged Dad to sell my cookies for me.

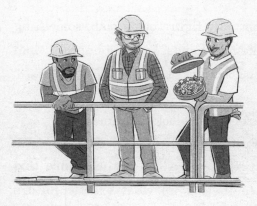

Scout life wasn't for me. Then there was a tumbling phase before I realized I really just wanted to run and jump into the pits of foam blocks instead of becoming a gymnast.

So, I have a reputation for being a little flaky in this department.

The first step is to figure out if I have any real skills. Maybe I'm good at something I don't even know yet. The possibility that there's something out there that I'm good at is as mysterious as it is exciting.

What if I could not only figure out a club, something to do after school like my friends, but *also* impress Mom with how responsible I am now? Like Caro.

"I'm going to join a smart kids' club."

"A what?" Caro asks, finally looking at me.

"Something like Future Leaders?" Mom asks.

"Exactly like Future Leaders!" I say excitedly, and make a mental note to look up what exactly Future Leaders is.

"¿Qué es eso?" Abuela asks, and I could almost kiss her.

"It's like a key club or honors society," Caro explains. "They volunteer around school, help teachers, mentor kids. Stuff like that." She looks at me again. "Really?"

"Yes, really. Seventh grade is all about figuring out who we are."

Abuela shoots me a wink and Mom smiles proudly like it was all her idea.

Maggie's plan to make seventh grade awesome!

CHAPTER 6

After dinner, I head upstairs and see that Abuela is already in my room. She sits at my desk with a radio that chatters away in Spanish. There's a mirror in front of her that she's leaning close to while wielding a pair of tweezers.

"What are you doing?" I ask, but my stomach drops when I see her pluck out a hair.

From her *chin*.

I curiously touch the soft skin over my lip. I do *not* have a mustache, but that tiny hair feels like a very ominous threat.

I climb onto my top bunk, where I open the laptop and log on to *BioBuild* to meet Julian. He's already online.

In the chat I type:

magpieOfmischief:
heyyy, I decided to
join a club
roboJellybean:
Cooooool
roboJellybean:
which club?

magpieOfmischief: future leaders

roboJellybean: really???

magpieOfmischief: YES RLY

magpieOfmischief: I can be a leader

roboJellybean: absolutely

roboJellybean: start by finishing that cactus maze u
started

roboJellybean: it's only a couple weeks until
commander bunny's stream!

magpieOfmischief: aye aye captain

roboJellybean: also check out the last killer loop I
just built

roboJellybean: but careful with the lava

The first Future Leaders meeting is on Friday and I wake
up early that morning—to the delight of Abuela—because

I know I need to look the part. Abuela irons my freshly laundered khaki shorts and dark blue polo shirt.

It's important to look professional. I learned that from Mom. She usually says this when I roll out of bed and forget to put on deodorant, but she is always sure to add that it's just as important to never lose your personal style in the pursuit of success.

I'm twelve years old. How in the world am I supposed to know what my style is? I'm only just now getting into the habit of remembering to wash my face before bed every night. And that's only because Abuela threatens me with her night cream when I don't. And that stuff smells like baby powder and medicine.

My uniform is looking sharp, but I have no idea how to tame my wavy hair. I usually just wear it loose or in a ponytail, but I'm a Future Leader now so I attempt one of Mom's buns.

It looks good. Different, but good. Is it my style, though? Caro loves her hoop earrings, baggy jeans, and sneakers. Dad knows he's a middle-aged punk rock kid from Miami and loves band tees. But as of right now, I have no clue about my style. Most days I still refer to a lot of the stuff in my closet as my play clothes. It's another thing about myself that I don't know.

Maybe instead of all these math and biology tests, we should be taking personality ones. I could pick my favorite season, school subject, and snack, and then some algorithm could just tell me everything

about myself so I wouldn't have to figure all this out on my own.

If I could figure out what I'm good at outside of playing video games, bothering Caro, and eating pastelitos, maybe then all this other stuff would fall into place.

I look at my whole outfit again and realize the Toddler Watch kind of ruins it. But still. Not bad. Baby steps. Or whatever the opposite of baby steps is.

When I meet Zoey and Julian at school, they are both very impressed with the sharp creases in my khakis.

Julian cups his hands around his mouth. "Respect the pleats!"

Zoey whistles. "Looking sharp and in charge!"

A little bit of ironing sure does seem to go a long way as far as productivity. I get a B on a pop quiz in English, and in PE, Coach Schwartz commends my posture.

When I get to art, Ms. Pérez informs me that I'm putting out great vibes today.

"Thanks," I tell her. "My abuela ironed my uniform."

She gives me a thumbs-up. "Impressive."

"Also, I'm going to be a Future Leader."

I'm sure Ms. Pérez understands dressing for the life we want. Her outfit screams Cool Middle School Art Teacher.

Our teacher last year was the *worst*. She once made me redo the sky in a picture because she said my turquoise coloring pencil was green, not blue.

But Ms. Pérez is all about learning new skills, but also exploring and having fun while expressing ourselves.

I wish that I could draw like Julian, because then I wouldn't need any personality test. I'd already have my "thing" and it would mean hanging out with him and Ms. Pérez. I could draw comics and have paint on my clothes, wear rainbow bracelets, and everyone would be like, *That's Maggie! She's such a great artist!*

But all I can manage are those loopy flowers. A shame since this tight bun is *really* starting to give me a headache.

The Future Leaders club meets in a classroom in the eighth-grade hall after school. Mrs. Giles is a tall Black woman from South Carolina. She has the best southern accent and today wears her braids tied up with a yellow headband. There are lots of posters of math puns on her classroom walls (*Are monsters good at math? Not unless you Count Dracula!*) and sunflowers on her desk.

"Welcome, young leaders. I'm so excited y'all are interested in our club. You'll each have many opportunities to serve as role models and mentors. Grades are important to continue membership, so that's something to keep in mind. Let me show you some of our first volunteer opportunities that you can start signing up for next week."

I study the whiteboard. Making this immediate choice feels like tumbling into yet another question about myself.

Summer or fall? Math or writing? Dogs or cats? Pizza or tacos? Ice cream or cupcakes? Pastelitos or croquetas?

My stomach is really feeling this longer stretch between lunch and home.

As far as sign-ups, Pen Pals with the nearby retirement community seems a popular choice. A new friend could be cool, but I'm really trying to focus on my current ones. Plus,

I already have an old person in my life. Beach Cleanup is right up my alley, though.

Maybe we can do something like that once Zoey and Julian have time to hang out at Dolphin Park again. But there's also Fall Festival, which is the best. I can almost taste the gooey cinnamon buns and feel that first hint of a breeze. Fall Fest always seems to happen during that first cold weather front of the year, when all of Miami brings out that one cute sweater that barely gets worn.

Someone steps up to the board next to me and I realize it's Eerie Eddie.

Eerie Eddie is a future leader? He tips his chin to acknowledge me. Has he always had a couple of hairs on his chin?

I pull the tie out of my bun, letting my wavy hair fall free. Eddie is a clear example that I don't need to be all buttoned-up for this. What a relief.

Outside the supermarket, Pablo waves when he sees me walking up to the busy window counter.

"Maggie! I've got something new for you to try!"

"Wow, it looks like a chocolate cloud!" I tell him, and dig in. I smile as the rich taste hits me. "It tastes like one, too!"

Pablo smiles. He dusts sugar from his hands and grabs my regular order of one guava pastelito and throws in a can of pineapple soda. "How was your day?" he asks.

I sigh and take a sip of my drink. "I joined a club."

His eyes light up. "Yeah? Which one?"

"Future Leaders." I set the can down on the counter. "I'm going to start volunteering. Become a mentor, clean up the beach, stuff like that."

"Wow, that's impressive!"

"Yeah, I'm in seventh grade now; it's time to become more responsible. And since I have to keep my grades up for the club and to get my phone, it's time to get super smart, too."

Pablo puts his hand over his heart. "You've always been super smart, Maggie."

I give him a skeptical look.

He gestures to the plate I just practically licked clean. "Have I ever steered you wrong?"

Pablo gives me a pastelito for the road. Being his official taster is a pretty great gig. When I get home, Mom seems tired from studying and Lucas's teething, but she listens to me talk about Future Leaders and tells me again how proud she is of me. I may not know my style yet, but I definitely know I'm on the right path.

Okay, so new step one: Figure out my first Future Leaders project.

Step two: Straight-A's Galaxy Brain.

CHAPTER 7

You might not know it by looking at me, but PE is my favorite class. Despite the sticky and hot Florida weather, and my body's insistence on sweating, there are two very important reasons why I love PE.

We're running laps today, which really means walking around the field together and talking until Coach Schwartz sees us and reminds us that we're in middle school and this isn't recess. Once we're out of his line of sight, we slow down again.

"How was Future Leaders?" Zoey asks me.

"Pretty cool. Mrs. Giles is the teacher in charge, and she is very chill. She didn't even make us do anything yet."

"Well, it was the first day," Zoey says.

"Yeah, but now that I think about it, it's weird how everyone was quiet and attentive. It was like—"

"They actually wanted to be there?" Julian finishes with a laugh. He tugs at his PE shirt. It's a hand-me-down from one of his older brothers, because with five boys, his mom refuses to buy a new set.

Unfortunately for Julian, he got way taller this summer, and now the faded shirt is a couple inches away from becoming a crop top.

"That's like band, too," Zoey says. "Sure, there's an occasional food fight, but it's fun. Clubs are way different than school."

I can't imagine the straitlaced Future Leaders kids being in a food fight, but then again, I only just met them. And Eerie Eddie *is* part of the club, so I probably shouldn't jump to any conclusions.

Julian looks at me. "Hey, don't forget to finish the maze."

Oh, yikes. I'd meant to log on to *BioBuild* and work on it yesterday.

Julian continues. "I'm finishing up the list of custom commands for the server. The spawn point for new players is going to be in the maze. It's going to be awesome."

I groan. "Are you giving me homework? *Not* chill."

Zoey laughs and Julian rolls his eyes. "Commander Bunny is visiting servers next month, and we have to be ready."

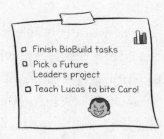

- ☐ Finish BioBuild tasks
- ☐ Pick a Future Leaders project
- ☐ Teach Lucas to bite Carol

I have to finish the maze, a haunted neighborhood, and the zombie pig farm. It's a lot of building, but it'll be fun.

We turn around, and Coach Schwartz's attention lasers in on us, but before he can call us out, we take off. One good thing about being seventh graders is learning from your sixth-grade mistakes.

Julian is huffing and puffing beside me. I'm a little winded but Zoey isn't breathing hard. She doesn't like to run, but she says that breath control is important when playing the flute.

I don't actually hate running. But I definitely miss the freedom of recess and playing games that didn't have to be competitions. We could role-play on the playground, doing all the weird voices, coming up with different games. We could just be silly and have fun.

But these days it feels like *everything* has to be for a reason.

The next Future Leaders meeting is on Friday. I ask Abuela to iron my uniform again, but this time, I lose the hair bun. These pleats are powerful, because not even a surprise pop quiz in math class gets me down.

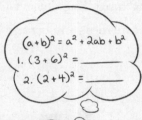

"Clear your desks, kids!"

I grab a sharpened pencil and settle in to take the quiz.

Apparently in seventh grade, we need to start learning pre-algebra topics. Equations and inequalities. Probability and polygons. Variables everywhere as they expect me to solve for the unknown.

My stomach sinks as I rush to hide my graded quiz in the very back of my folder. I don't

even want to go over what I got wrong. I quickly snap my binder closed.

"You okay?" Zoey asks from the desk next to me. I spot her quiz on her folder. A 98 percent.

I nod and try to smile.

One good thing is I have time to get my overall grade up over the next couple of weeks if I can stay on top of my homework. Maybe there will also be chances to get extra credit.

One disappointing quiz does not decide a report card.

The second the dismissal bell rings, I rush toward the eighth-grade hall and Mrs. Giles's classroom. I'm one of the first to arrive. I march right up to the whiteboard and write my name under Beach Cleanup, Library Shelving Project, *and* Fall Festival.

Saved by the smart kids' club.

CHAPTER 8

The beach cleanup is on Saturday, so I dedicate my Friday night to working on the maze in our *BioBuild* server. But I'm distracted and annoyed that it's not coming out how I planned.

Also, it's really hard to focus when Abuela is watching her evening telenovela at my desk *soooo* loud while she knits. A really wild Friday night.

I lean over the edge of the bunk.

"Abuela, can you please lower that?" I ask.

"¿Qué?"

"The TV," I say, and point at it.

"Ah," she says, and lowers the volume. Misunderstanding what I meant, she proceeds to spend the next ten minutes catching me up on the ridiculous drama. Despite myself, I become interested in characters I've known for only ten minutes.

"But he married her sister!" I complain.

"¡Es un descarado!"

Caro stops by my bedroom. She leans against the open door with a smirk.

I see you have big Friday night plans.

I make a mental note, reminding myself of my plan to teach Lucas to bite her.

Caro turns her smile on Abuela and asks to borrow her car.

"¿Adónde vas, Caro?" Abuela asks her.

"A friend's house."

Abuela narrows her eyes. This isn't her Tienes un Novio alarm.

This is the And Where Do You Think You're Going siren. A classic.

"Pero qué friend's house, ni qué friend's house?" Abuela asks.

The question is a trap. Amused, I settle in to watch.

Caro turns her innocent smile on Abuela. "It's a study group, Abuela."

I roll my eyes. There's no way Abuela will believe her.

"¿Solamente niñas?"

Caro's smile brightens. "Yup, just us girls."

Abuela plucks the keys out of her giant purse and hands them to my sister. Caro circles them around her finger in the air before leaving to go drive in Miami's really bad traffic. Meanwhile, I'm barely able to ride my bike to a nearby park.

I'm about to complain about my life drama when I notice Abuela's suddenly sad expression.

"You okay, Abuela?"

She's quiet for a second, but then she nods. The commercial ends and her telenovela comes back on, so she focuses on the little TV.

Abuela has lived with us for two months now. Abuelo was sick for a long time, and she quit her job to take care of him. But after he died, she sold their old house in Homestead to move in with us. She looks really cramped and uncomfortable at my desk. Dad is building her a tiny house in our backyard. He calls it an in-law suite. He's supposed to finish it when he gets back next month. Well, that's what he says. I bet Abuela wants her own room as much as I want my room back.

"Everything will be better as soon as Dad gets home," I tell her.

I don't think Abuela hears me because she doesn't say anything.

My alarm wakes me on Saturday morning. Time to clean some beaches. I fly out of bed and pull on one of Dad's shirts and a pair of jean shorts. I twist my hair up into a loose bun and check myself in the mirror. I turn one way, then the other. This could be my style.

When Mom sees me, she smiles. "You look like your dad. Very cute!"

"Did you go to any of these concerts with Dad?" I ask, pulling out my shirt to read the band name. They wore a *lot* of eyeliner back then.

"I sure did," Mom says. "He wasn't the only punk rock kid."

That former so-called *punk rock kid* shoves a very heavy bag into my arms.

"I'm not going to the beach to have a picnic," I tell her as I pick through the packed lunch, extra snacks, sunscreen, and giant jug of water. "I'm going to clean it up, Mom. This is serious business."

"And you have to be nice and hydrated to pick up all that garbage," she says.

"People who litter are the worst," Caro says, and I don't

argue, because she's not wrong. I was too distracted last night to finish the maze, so I watched videos about sea turtles, which led me to watching videos about manatees and dolphins and all the junk that ends up in oceans and rivers. I woke up mad and ready to save our beaches.

Today, we're cleaning the beach at Dolphin Park. I almost ask Mom for a trial run of my bike privileges, but since I have to carry this bag, I decide not to push for it yet.

She hasn't said no, so I'm hopeful. I'm also pumped to help clean the beach and save some sea turtles. I'm so pumped that it doesn't even bother me that Caro is the one tasked with driving me.

But when we get there, I spot Coach Schwartz assisting Mrs. Giles and the volunteers. When my PE teacher sees Caro, he smiles for the first time I've ever seen. I didn't even know his face could do that.

"Carolina Diaz! What are you doing here?" he asks.

"Hey, Coach! Just dropping off my sister."

Coach Schwartz looks at me like he doesn't quite remember who I am.

Before Caro and Coach Schwartz start reminiscing about her glory days in cross-country at West Memorial, I shoo her away by reminding her she was on her way to get iced coffee. Other than school competitions, nothing gets my sister moving faster than iced coffee.

The sea breeze is welcome on such a hot morning. I'm slathered in sunscreen and ready to work. I stand with the rest of the group.

Again, I'm surprised to see Eddie. This doesn't seem to be his scene. Outside, that is. He's got a white stripe of sunscreen spread across his nose and is also wearing a black T-shirt and pants.

"Cool shirt," he says.

"Thanks." I don't tell him it's actually my dad's. Actually, come to think of it, I bet he and Dad would love the same music.

"Are you excited?" I ask him.

He shrugs. "I'm just here for the sea turtles."

I nod, impressed. "That's cool."

Coach Schwartz greets us in a big, booming voice before pointing out the stretch of beach we'll be cleaning. We get started and I'm both annoyed to see garbage and excited to pick it up. As I drop each piece in my bag, it really hits me that I'm doing something important.

The sun is shining, the sea breeze is warm, and I'm doing something productive and important on a weekend. This Future Leader business was such a good idea.

My watch sings out with a message. I forgot to silence it this morning. The song sounds like someone stepped on a kid's toy.

I roll my eyes and send back a quick *Ok!* (the watch offers a handful of auto-replies) but when I look up, I notice the three eighth graders are staring at me.

They're looking at me the way everyone looks at Lucas when he babbles some new sound. But they're not looking at me like I'm some adorable miracle of a baby boy.

They're looking at me like I'm a seventh-grade baby.

I. Hate. This. Watch.

I stab my picker-up stick thing in a Styrofoam cup. Eerie Eddie stops beside me. He glances at me and then at the sand in front of us. He plucks up the other soda cup in front of me.

"You have to be faster than that, Diaz."

"What?"

He picks up another piece of discarded trash. It feels like a challenge. I smirk and hurry ahead to collect as much trash as I can. Eddie is on my heels as he does the same.

At the end of the day, we've picked up the most. I decide to ignore the eighth graders who made me feel bad and focus on that.

"Are you volunteering for Fall Festival, too?" I ask Eddie, and he nods.

He doesn't talk much, but it's nice to feel like I sort of have a friend in this club. And since he doesn't make fun of my watch, I split the ham sandwich Mom made me with him.

* CHAPTER 9 *

At lunch on Monday, Zoey latches onto my arm, her eyes wide. "I need your advice." She yanks off her headphones and hands them to me. "Listen and give me your honest opinion. Julian is too nice."

Across the table, Julian continues to sketch and eat his lunch. "I'm a positive person," he says. He squints at us before shoving a handful of tots into his mouth and returning to his sketch pad. "Can you turn toward the sunlight a little?"

"What are you doing?" I ask him.

"Forget him," Zoey says, and I can't even get a word in before she yanks her headphones down over my ears and hits play. I immediately recognize the sound of her flute playing.

"It's me practicing with Maya and her friends," she explains, pulling one headphone away from my ear.

"When did you play with them?"

"Friday after band practice," she says. "I think they want me to play with them at the Fall Festival talent show."

"Wow," I say slowly, feeling like I'm trying to catch up.

"Stop moving so much, Zoey," Julian complains, hunched over his drawing.

Zoey ignores him, focused on me. "I recorded my parts, because you know I have to hear what you think."

She lets go of the headphone and it pops back over my ear, canceling out every other sound. Zoey twists her hands nervously as she watches me closely, waiting for a reaction. Zoey is used to being good at stuff. Her straight-A streak is so long that her mom had to move the report cards off the fridge.

She's been busy hanging out with ultra-cool Mambo Maya, but what I think still matters to her. It makes me feel good. Even though I'm not a musician, she still wants to hear my opinion. It's her way of including me.

"It sounds great," I tell her honestly.

"Really?" she asks, sounding worried.

"Would I lie?"

Julian laughs, and when I try to steal a glance at his sketchbook, he pulls it away. "Uh-uh, not yet."

"Since when can't I look at your comic?" I ask, surprised.

"It's not my comic. It's the concept we're working on for the mural!"

"Wait, *what*?" When did all of this happen? It's only been a weekend!

"Ms. Pérez told us that our art club got approved for a mural!" Julian says happily.

"Where?" Zoey asks.

"Right by the bakery!"

Julian tells us that Ms. Pérez is planning a big presentation to show it off once it's done. It's great news, but it feels like there's a deflating balloon in my chest. Zoey is going to play with Mambo Maya in the talent show, and Julian is painting a mural the whole city will see. And me? I'm missing everything *again*.

Beach Cleanup was fun and Future Leaders is a great way to prove myself to Mom. But is any of that what I love to do?

My latest Future Leaders project is helping our school's library weed out old books that stink like mildew and shelve new ones. It's pretty mindless work, except for a paper cut or two and getting distracted by the interesting books.

September is almost over, which means our first progress reports will be given out soon. But first is next week's Fall Festival. I have to help teachers organize volunteers and prepare for different events. Multitasking is the worst, but I've got no time to complain. Volunteering is taking up so much of my after-school time. Plus, I have to make sure any sneaky pop quizzes don't ruin my grades. My current to-do list could compete against Mom's.

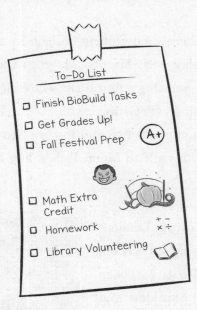

To-Do List

☐ Finish BioBuild Tasks
☐ Get Grades Up! (A+)
☐ Fall Festival Prep

☐ Math Extra
   Credit
☐ Homework   + −
                    × ÷
☐ Library Volunteering 📖

Mom's been studying so much for all of her classes. She graduates in December, and she's definitely getting more stressed the closer we get to the end of the semester.

I can relate. I've been so busy that I haven't even had to *try* to stay out of her hair.

It's not just Mom and me who are hustling away. Caro goes to cross-country most mornings and then track meets on the weekends. And whenever I finally have time to hang out with Zoey and Julian, instead of doing something fun together, we're all focused on something else.

Only Abuela seems to be the one with nothing new or exciting to do lately.

She watches Lucas during the day so Mom can go to class. And then she gives him his evening bath so Mom can focus on studying once she gets home. Abuela also makes sure we all stop everything we're doing to actually eat a real dinner. But then she slips quietly into my room to watch the news or an episode of one of her telenovelas.

Seems pretty boring to me.

I log on to *BioBuild* to finish the maze and get started on the zombie pig farm I'm *super* behind on. It's time to check some more stuff off my list. Commander Bunny's stream is the Saturday after Fall Festival. That's more than a week away, so there's still plenty of time.

To get my tasks on the server done.

And all the homework I'm behind on because of volunteering.

It's still two weeks until progress reports.

And Dad coming home to finish Abuela's suite.

And . . .

⋆ CHAPTER 10 ⋆

West Memorial Middle's Fall Festival is always a ton of fun, even when I had to tag along with Caro and her friends because Mom made her take me. Last year was the first time I got to roam free with Zoey and Julian. The three of us played all the carnival games our combined allowances could get us. Then we ate arepas stuffed with cheese so melty it stretched perfectly whenever we tore one in half.

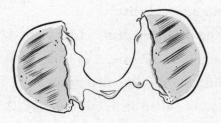

And this year, as a volunteer I get to skip my last classes on Friday to help set up with the other Future Leaders before the festival opens after school.

Turns out responsibility sometimes comes with serious perks.

No wonder Caro is so annoyingly perfect.

I meet Eerie Eddie outside Mrs. Giles's class and he hands me a heavy box packed full of reams of tickets. I imagine all the carnival games a person could play with them and my brain almost shorts out.

"You need to get those to the front office."

I realize I'm breathing hard as I hold the box tighter to my chest. "So many tickets."

"Calm down, Gollum." He drops a list on top of the box.

It's yet another to-do list.

I'm running from one corner of school to the other when my watch starts to vibrate. (No song to embarrass me again. This time, I remembered to silence it.) I check it to reply to whatever Mom sent, but see that it's the low battery warning.

In all the chaos, I forgot to charge it this week. Oops!

"Maggie, the pumpkins!" Coach Schwartz calls, and I

FALL FEST

①

Deliver tickets.

②

Move pumpkins.

③

Set up mystery boxes.

④

Assist with the petting zoo.

 ⑤ Get ticket money!

  ⑥ Meet up with Zoey before talent show!

hurry to the pickup truck loaded with pumpkins to be decorated at the carving station.

I'm basically a delivery girl, and it's a *lot* of work. After the pumpkins, I have to cut out openings in cardboard boxes that will become monster mystery boxes as soon as I fill them with their gross contents. (Cooked spaghetti as brains! Peeled grapes as eyeballs! Corn as loose monster teeth!)

I'm so busy after dismissal (which is *so* weird) that I don't even have time to meet up with my friends before the festival like we did last year.

Beeeeeeeeeeeeep.

On my wrist, my watch finally dies.

"Oh no!" I click the buttons, wishing for the first time ever for it to turn on.

"Petting zoo, Maggie!" Eerie Eddie tells me as he runs past with the speakers for the talent show stage.

"But I have a goat allergy," I shout after him. I don't, but *ugh*. So many smells.

Eerie Eddie doesn't even slow down. "Nice try."

Two hours later, the sun begins to set and the school track fills up with booths and games. I'm sweaty and hungry, but it's so cool seeing this year's Fall Festival come to life. I feel accomplished and pretty proud of my work.

I find Zoey outside the auditorium, where the talent show will start soon.

"There you are!" She runs up to me with her flute case. "What do you think about my outfit?"

She looks amazing, and I tell her that. She also matches with Maya and all her friends while I'm a gross, frazzled mess. They look so cool and it's Zoey's total dream. And part of the reason I even volunteered for the festival was so I could be here to see Zoey.

So why do I have a stomachache all of a sudden?

"You're going to watch the talent show, right?" Zoey asks. "I saved you a seat."

I think, *Of course I will!* But what I say is "I'll definitely try."

Being wishy-washy about this surprises me, too.

Zoey's face falls. "What? You're not going to watch?" Mambo Maya and her crew move closer to stand around Zoey. As her best friend, it makes me want to stand even closer to Zoey, but I'm afraid I might smell like goat.

"It's just that I'm really busy," I explain.

It doesn't make sense to feel left out. Zoey has been practicing and hanging out with Maya since August and I don't even play an instrument.

"It's fine, whatever," Zoey says. "You've been really busy lately."

"You were busy first!" I accuse her.

Zoey shakes her flute case. "Doing what I love, Maggie." She spins away, and Mambo Maya and the rest of their band go with her.

Eerie Eddie races past me, carrying tickets and painted pumpkins. "Maggie, help!"

I hurry after Eddie with my still unfinished to-do list. Knowing Zoey is mad at me ruins everything, and these tasks don't feel fun or important anymore. Because Zoey's right. She's doing what she loves, while I've been running around being busy doing new, random things to find what *I* love. But shelving at the library and being everyone's delivery girl doesn't feel like a passion. It definitely doesn't scream *Maggie Diaz*.

I drop my list and race off to find Julian so we can watch Zoey together.

But I find Caro instead.

"She hasn't—" I start to argue, but then look at my wrist. My watch is totally dead.

"Oh *no* . . ." I slowly say. This is more terrifying than anything I could have put in those monster mystery boxes.

Caro nods furiously. "Oh *yeah*. Mami's going to kill you."

★ CHAPTER 11 ★

It's time for another family *conversation*, and this time I am the star of the show.

The promise of great grades won't get me out of this one. Charts, graphs, and reminders about me selflessly sharing my room can't save me. Nothing will make up for the most terrible of mistakes.

Because for almost an hour, my Cuban mother had no idea where I was.

"Magdalena Victoria—"

Not only my full first name. She's middle-naming me, too. I'm doomed.

What's your phone number?

I'm not allowed to have a phone.

I am *never* getting an actual phone. And I'll never be able to bike to Dolphin Park.

"My watch died," I say again, but it's useless. Despite panicking over my location for that past hour, Mom does *not* want to hear my voice now.

And because the world is upside down, Caro is the one coming to my defense.

"She was at school," Caro points out as she paces from one end of the kitchen to the other.

Mom shakes her head.

"The responsibilities of after-school activities are new for Maggie," Caro reasons. "And Maggie is not known for remembering things."

"Hey now," I complain.

Caro shoots me a look and I go silent.

Mom finally discovered my location after calling school, where she reached someone who was sure they had seen me helping set up the mystery boxes. But that one hour proved my mom right on all of her worries.

"This just proves how much I do need a real phone," I say in a small voice, out of sheer desperation.

Mom considers me for a long moment before coming to her verdict.

"Seeing as this is your first major offense and you *were* at school . . ."

I'm not only back to where I started, I am flung even further back.

Caro nods. "That's fair."

I sit up quickly, but Caro shoots me another sharp look. This is the best I'll get.

I trudge back to my room and watch Mom take the laptop.

"One month," Mom says with finality.

I'm officially cut off.

I wake up on Saturday and for a split second I'm happy because it's my favorite day of the week. Except then I remember all the trouble I'm in. Mom's quiet, which I hate, so I mostly hang out in my room with Abuela, which is about as cool as it sounds. Abuela tries to show me how to knit and it's frustrating. But with nothing else to do, I stick with it. After a while it starts to feel a little bit like a matching game or something.

It keeps my hands and head busy, which I'm grateful for, because it's better than enduring the silent treatment from Mom or panicking over all the headway I've lost when it comes to her considering me responsible enough to earn some real independence.

I won't be knitting anything useful anytime soon, but this is Miami, and it's not like we'd ever get to wear a scarf anyway.

Sunday promises to be just as boring until I hear a very familiar voice.

DAD'S HOME!!!

I race out of my room and right into his arms. He drops his bag and lets out a huff and a laugh as he squeezes me back. I've missed him so much. There are about a hundred reasons why Dad being home makes everything better.

The most important is Mom's obvious better mood.

I also missed his jokes.

Introduction of Dad!

Don't trust atoms!

They make up everything!

And with Dad back home, it means he'll get back to work on Abuela's tiny house, which also means me *finally* getting my room back.

He lets go of me to kiss Mom, which is gross, but obviously makes her happy. And I'm a fan of anything that makes Mom happier right now.

"I love seeing these adorable mugs!" he says. "All right, everyone, tell me everything I missed in the next ten seconds," he jokes.

Dad's work is like being a tow truck driver, but for wrecks and accidents that happen out in the middle of the ocean. He also helps move and deliver huge pieces of cargo from one harbor to another. I like when he goes on those trips, because it means I get a ridiculous souvenir from some beach town up north somewhere.

MIAMI

And so many places are up north somewhere when you're from Miami.

Since he had to go all the way to Maine this time, he brought Mom nice candles, fancy coffee for Abuela, and for Caro and me, shirts that say COOL AS A MOOSE. I immediately put mine on and Dad cheers, delighted.

We crowd around the table for dinner and it's as cramped as I thought it would be. But with yesterday, I'm glad to have Dad home. Mom's also happy. The house is starting to feel normal again.

We're all super excited, talking over one another to get Dad's attention. Caro tells him about her track meets and weird noises the car makes whenever she drives it and other boring things. Finally, I yank the spotlight to me.

"I've been volunteering after school," I tell him, and quickly check Mom to make sure she's not about to rat me out or get mad all over again, but she's feeding Lucas. "And I'm about to get a killer report card."

"Maggie Diaz, on the honor roll!" Dad sings, his eyes bright, giving me a high five.

"Well, not yet," I hedge.

"What kind of volunteering?" he asks.

I strategically decide to skip over Fall Festival. "I've been helping our school library with shelving, and also beach cleanup over at Dolphin Park."

"That's great, Maggie. I love that park," Dad says.

I jump right into that awesome opening. "Me too! Mom said I can start riding my bike there if my grades are good."

"Magdalena," Mom says in a low warning voice, and Dad's eyes widen.

"Uh-oh," he jokes.

Not wanting Mom to sour the moment and bring up my grounding, I hurry on. "And I was thinking I can help more around the house. I can work with you to finish Abuela's tiny house!"

"Finally, huh?" Dad asks with a laugh.

My dad is very funny and plays video games and is pretty chill, but it can also take him *forever* to finish things. It drives my mom up the wall how Dad will start a project and jump to the next one without finishing the first.

I glance at Abuela, whose spot at the table has shifted with Dad's return. She's squeezed in closer to Lucas's

FINISH PAINTING SHED

Don't worry, I got this!

FIX BROKEN PIPE

CLEAN GUTTERS

FINISH GARDEN TILING

high chair, even though Dad offered to take that chair and leave her at the head of the table.

"Ay, no te preocupes," she told him. "Tú eres el papá."

I don't know why him being our dad means that's automatically his seat, but maybe he called shotgun infinity before I was born.

Dad turns his bright smile on Abuela and asks her in Spanish if I'm still a slob.

Abuela.smiles a little and shoots me a quick wink.

"I'm sure Abuela is tired of being roommates," I say.

Abuela continues to quietly eat. She's not in on Mom and

Dad's jokes or jumping into our conversations. Instead, she's pushing the rice on her plate around like Caro does whenever she's moody.

Something about Abuela's sullen mood makes me feel like I shouldn't be *too* obvious about my impatience for independence.

"Clubs? Honor roll? Helping out around the house? You're killing it," Dad tells me, and I beam thanks to the praise. Dad being home really makes everything better.

I take a short bow from my seat.

"And no more speeding tickets for Carolina?" he asks.

MORE?!

Dad laughs louder than I expect. *"I'm kidding!* You know me," he says, and then hurries to finish his dinner.

Later that night, after I've showered and brushed my teeth, I slip into my room. Abuela is at my desk, applying her night cream. This one smells really sweet and powdery, like SweeTarts. She rubs it down her neck without looking at me.

"Good night, Abuela." I climb up into my bunk.

"Buenas noches, Magdalena," Abuela returns quietly, and flips off the light.

I get under my blanket, but then toss and turn until she clicks on her humidifier, and I realize the quiet hum is a sound I'm getting used to at night now.

I am about to close my eyes when I notice Abuela pick up the small picture frame on my desk. It's a picture of her and Abuelo. I get a tight feeling in my chest and my eyes burn. I miss him and his big,  round laugh and how he always smelled like vanilla and cherry because of his cigars.

Abuela looks at the picture for a long time before putting it down and getting into bed.

★ CHAPTER 12 ★

"¡Levántate, Magdalena, vas a llegar tarde a la escuela!"

Abuela's routine wake-up call is welcome this morning. It erases the weird sinking feeling from last night. I get dressed and put on my charged watch.

Today is a big day. Progress cards will be issued. And with Dad home, I'm feeling hopeful and confident again. Honor Roll Maggie can *totally* fix this blip.

I skip into the kitchen, where I find Mom drinking her coffee with Dad. "Progress reports today," I inform her.

"I'm excited to see it, Maggie," she says, and I'm relieved to no longer be Magdalena Victoria.

Dad shoots back his coffee. "Ah, so good. I love being home."

"And we sure love having you here." I rub my hands together. "When do we get started on Abuela's tiny house? I'm ready to get my tool belt."

"Don't I get a couple days off?" he asks, laughing. "I just got home."

Caro walks in with a homemade iced coffee. To save money, Abuela has started making them for her every morning.

Caro looks at Dad. "Please do not give her a hammer."

"No promises," Dad jokes, then grabs his keys. "But I will give her a ride to school."

I don't mind riding my bike, but I also love riding with Dad because he always blasts his music super loud. His playlists are filled with bands from when he was a teenager, and those songs had a *lot* of screaming. But that's what makes it so funny to watch him sing along.

I jump out of the car once he stops in the car loop. "Thanks for the ride, Dad." I have to shout this, because he's still playing his music. Teachers glance over. Dad cheerfully waves at them.

"Honor Roll Maggie," he calls out, and my confidence jumps.

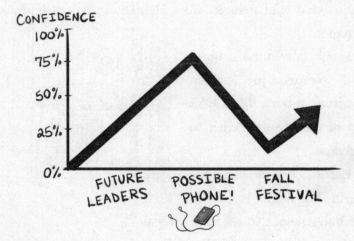

As I head to meet Zoey and Julian, the bell rings, and I realize that I'm *way* later than I thought since Dad took the long, very noisy way to school.

I hurry to homeroom and make it to my desk just in time.

No tardy slip yet for me, thank you very much.

Behind me, Eerie Eddie sneezes. I jerk around to look at him. He rolls his eyes. "It's my allergies."

"Okay, everyone, we're nine weeks into school and you know what that means." Mrs. Delgado pulls out a stack of paper.

I rub my hands again and picture my golden progress report. My ticket out of trouble and back to freedom.

Eerie Eddie sneezes again. The sound is a high-pitched squeal. "Can I have a tissue?"

I'm closest to the shelf, so I reach over and toss him one, never taking my eyes off Mrs. Delgado, who's moving around the room alphabetically. I should be soon.

Thank you, *D* for Diaz.

I can't wait to be back on track to getting my phone. I'll be able to text Julian and Zoey after school. Which means we'll hang out *way* more. I'll know about new songs, not just my dad's old jams. I'll download apps and take cute pictures. Of me. Other people's dogs. Maybe of whatever scarf I end up knitting. It'll be awesome!

I unfold it to see the graph of grades. My own phone! My room back! Pastelitos at the beach with my best friends!

Behind me, Eerie Eddie sneezes again.

"Are you kidding me?" I shout.

"I'm sorry," Eddie says. "I swear it's just allergies!"

My heart is pounding as I walk to my next period. I've got tunnel vision. *D* is not for Diaz. *D* is for math.

When I get to lunch, I'm desperate to see my friends.

I need to talk to Zoey and Julian about all the things I can't at home.

When I get to our spot, I see Julian.

"I've got the worst news." I glance around. "Where's Zoey?"

Julian kicks the toe of his shoe against the sidewalk. "She had to meet up with Maya."

My shoulders fall as an angry wave twists my stomach into a knot. "She's *always* with Maya now."

"Not always," Julian argues.

Just over his shoulder, I see Zoey walking off with her new group. She doesn't even look back.

"Yes, she is!" I nearly shout. "I really need her right now, but she's with Maya *again*. She told me I was always busy lately, but she's practically dumped us."

"She was working on the talent show with Maya."

"But the show's over!"

Julian crosses his arms. I think he's mad at her, too, until he says, "And you didn't even go, Maggie."

And that's when it hits me. I missed Zoey's performance.

My heart speeds up. "Is she mad at me?"

He shrugs. "She was definitely disappointed, but I think they're just talking about band stuff now."

"I didn't mean to miss it," I explain. "Caro showed up and—"

"And you missed Saturday's event, too."

"Saturday?" I ask, confused.

And by his disappointed expression, I suddenly remember what else I forgot. The Saturday after Fall Festival. It was on my list! Oh no. Oh, no, no, *no*.

"Commander Bunny?" I ask in a small voice.

Julian's head falls back on a heavy sigh. "They immediately left our server after they spawned in the middle of a blocked-off maze they couldn't get out of."

"My mom grounded me," I hurry to explain. "If I had my own phone—"

"Yeah, yeah, I *know*," he cuts me off. "You and this magical phone."

"Well, this is what happens without one! I get grounded and then no one can reach me." Why can't anyone see that everything would be better if I had one? Once I get one, everything else will work out.

"Well, I gotta go," he tells me.

"You're not going to eat lunch?"

"Orthodontics appointment." He bares his teeth in a grimace before heading past me to the front office.

With Julian gone, and Zoey hanging out with other friends, I'm alone. Everyone else is already grouped up, their tables picked out and established. I glance around and notice a table by the brick wall. I spot another loner eating on their own.

I walk up to Eerie Eddie. "Can I sit here?"

He shrugs but moves his backpack out of the way for me.

We only have ten minutes left of lunch, and I don't have anything to eat, because I forgot to get in line. *Another* thing I forgot to do.

I probably look pathetic because Eddie offers me the other half of his quesadilla.

As I slowly eat, I try to reevaluate my plan.

I need to fix my grades ASAP. Zoey is mad and Julian

is disappointed, and Mom doesn't really need to see this progress report since it doesn't require a parent's signature like report cards do.

I can still fix everything.

I just have to keep my head down and make it to the end of the semester. I'll help Dad actually finish his to-do list. That'll show Mom how capable I am. And as a huge bonus, I'll get my bedroom back.

I have no idea how to build or fix stuff . . . but I could learn!

★ CHAPTER 13 ★

I'm starting to carefully time my morning arrival to make sure I get to school right as the bell rings. I keep my eyes on my watch—like a spy—but not in a cool way. Not having our usual morning hangout makes me feel like a stray, and I really don't want to awkwardly linger around now that Zoey's spending her mornings in the band room. She's not *not* talking to me, since we still sit next to each other in math and see each other at PE, but it's different

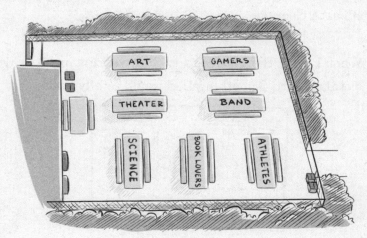

and weird. I hate it. She's sitting with the band kids at lunch now. I don't even have Julian, who had to get his lunch period switched this month because of some kind of gifted student testing he has to do. He's been quieter lately—distracted by his sketch for the mural—but he's probably mad at me, just like everyone else.

All the worrying is giving me a serious stomachache. I don't want to make Zoey madder, but I almost wish we'd had an actual big fight instead of whatever we are now. I don't know how to fix this. And unlike her, I don't have another group or team to sit with.

But at least I have Eerie Eddie? When I accidentally call him that during a Future Leaders meeting, my face burns. But he only smirks a little.

"It fits," he says with a shrug. "And you're Moody Maggie."

I laugh and we both decide to sign up for another round of beach cleanup.

When I get to the woodshop, it's like walking into a heavy metal concert. Something Dad would totally love.

INTRODUCTION MEETING

WOOD WORK CLUB

① Build projects designed to teach woodworking skills and shop safety

② Learn fundamentals of basic hand and power tool skills with the help of local artists.

This room is . . . loud.

There's a lot of sharp, menacing tools. Someone in the back is using an electric saw that screams and shrieks, and the whole place smells like the hardware store. The room has real danger vibes.

I go to stand with the other new members in a corner. The woodshop classroom is not a place I've ever visited. All I know about this program is that the students who are part of it have made furniture that has won contests that get written about in the newspaper.

"Welcome, everyone. I'm Mr. Santiago, and this is my kingdom." He laughs at his joke and I start to relax. I glance past him at all the tools and notice someone working on a surfboard. Whoa! Forget shelving, I want to make one of those.

Or I could make my own skateboard, since Mom won't let me ride Dad's longboard anymore. Last time Dad let me borrow it, I flew down the hilly road while sitting and gripping for dear life onto the sides. When I leaned to the right to turn, my knuckles skidded across the pavement.

Dad took me right to the ER. Mom banished the longboard.

But it would be totally different this time. I would actually stand up on the board.

Look, Mom, no hands!

"Maggie Diaz, are you listening?"

FWUP!

I glance around and realize everyone is looking at me. I take a shot in the dark and say, "Safety first?"

"Safety *always*. We want to keep all the digits we walked in here with, right?"

He laughs again. It sounds a little threatening this time.

"Introductory woodshop is a program that you can take in sixth and seventh grade after school. We make everything from shelves and tables to key chains, and yes, even surfboards. We will introduce

more advanced builds in the eighth grade. That's when we get to make some really fun stuff." Mr. Santiago gestures to the back wall.

It's like a museum to woodworking.

"Sometimes students even get to keep the pieces they've built. I've invited some former students to share some of their favorite pieces. They're here to answer all your questions, so don't be afraid to ask, but please be sure to stay safe and watch those hands."

WOODWORKING	
PROS	CONS
—Help Dad!	— Scary tools
— Get Abuela out of my room	— Loss of limb a strong possibility 😳
— Make my own skateboard	

I head past the saws and drills—and the reasonable furniture pieces—straight to the surfboard. It's bright blue with yellow flowers and *way* taller than me. And it definitely looks used. I've never surfed before, but I do love my skimboard.

SKIM

One of Mr. Santiago's former students walks up to me. "Hi! I'm Alex."

"Is that your surfboard?" I ask her.

"Yup," she says proudly. "I made it in this very workshop when I was in the eighth grade."

"Wow." I look from the surfboard to her. She looks Caro's age. "What grade are you in now?"

"Eleventh."

"Do you know my sister? Carolina Diaz?"

Her eyes widen. "You must be Maggie!"

That's weird. "How did you know that?"

"Caro's a really good friend of mine."

I realize this is Caro's new favorite friend, Alex.

Alex shows me around. She knows a *lot* about wood-working. She's also funny, and doesn't make me feel silly or like a baby when I ask her a million questions.

"You should really think about signing up for wood-working," Alex tells me at the end of the meeting. "You can make it what you want, you know?"

"What do you mean?"

"You get to learn skills, but whatever you want to make with them is up to you."

It reminds me of picking projects in Future Leaders.

"I've been trying to figure out what I'm into. My passion, you know?"

Mr. Santiago offers each of us a form for our parents to sign if we're interested. I hurry to his side to take one.

Out in the hallway, I catch up with Alex. "I just need to find something that defines me," I say, thinking of Julian with art, and Zoey with band.

"You're putting a lot of pressure on yourself," she says. "An extracurricular like woodshop is a lot of work."

"Caro told me you do *lots* of stuff."

We head outside to the parking lot. "I guess I do. But I play soccer and surf because I like to. Same reason I tutor. But I don't think any of that necessarily defines me."

Easy to say for someone who participates in sports and tutoring, *and* built her own surfboard in the eighth grade. She just doesn't get it.

We reach Caro's car, waiting in the car loop. As I open the passenger side, she's already complaining.

"Wow, that took forever. What were you—*Alex!*" she shrieks. She immediately tries to control her voice and sound cool. "What are you doing here?"

"I was here for the woodshop intro," Alex tells her.

"Right!" Caro says. Her voice is all high and squeaky. Not like the grumpy growl she just used on me. "I totally forgot."

I toss my backpack into the car. "Cool surfboard, Alex. Thanks for showing me around so *patiently*." I glare at Caro.

"No problem," Alex says. "And good luck on figuring out your passion. Just don't put *too* much pressure on it to be one thing."

Despite my struggles, I'm not *totally* clueless about life.

When Caro gets back in the car, I smirk at her.

"What?" she says in a hiss. Now that the cool girl is gone, ghoulish big sister is back.

"You *like* her," I say.

Caro rolls her eyes but says nothing. The blush is still there. Aw, how cute. Caro likes Alex!

After dinner, Abuela isn't in my room. I go outside and find her sitting on the front porch knitting. Now that it's October, the nights aren't as humid. I dig in her bag for my lumpy scarf and her extra needles.

"Do you have any hobbies, Abuela?" I ask.

"Claro," she says. "Me gusta ir de compras."

I laugh. "Shopping isn't a hobby."

Abuela grins, then points her lips at the clicking and clacking knitting needles in her hands. "Me gusta tejer y coser." There are knitted socks and doilies all over my bedroom.

"Hice vestidos cuando era más joven," she goes on.

"You made your own dresses?" I didn't know that. I glance down at my outfit and wonder if I could ever learn to make my own clothes.

Abuela nods, her hands smoothly flying. The ball of yarn beside her slowly unfurls.

"Y yo tenía un jardín."

She sounds a little sad when she says this, and I remember her garden and all the bright flowers that bloomed outside her and Abuelo's old house.

"Maybe we could start one here," I tell her.

It might not be as cool as surfing or building my own skateboard, but I know it'll make her happy.

✶ CHAPTER 14 ✶

Seventh grade isn't going to last forever, so I decide to leap right into the deep end of woodworking.

"I want to make a skateboard," I announce at the next meeting.

"Whoa," Mr. Santiago says with a laugh. "That one seems simple but is a doozy."

"I'm not here to glue Popsicle sticks together," I tell him.

"I see that, but let's start with something just a little easier, so you don't get overwhelmed."

A banana holder? Really? What kind of—? That's not fun or cool! Who in the world would ever want a banana holder?

Mr. Santiago takes the newcomers aside and goes through shop safety and proper tool handling with us. We all put on gloves and safety goggles. As beginners, we only have access to the hand tools. Hammers, screwdrivers, sandpaper. Mr. Santiago uses the saw to cut me a circle for the base of my banana holder.

I can't stop saying banana holder and laughing as I work.

But it's fine. I'll make this, gift it to Abuela (bonus points!), and then I'll level up to power tools and skateboards.

¡Ay, qué bueno!

Big fan of bananas and plantains

I hurry to finish my first project now, so I won't have to wait until next week to move on. I hammer a nail, then yank it out to make a hole. I stick the hook in place and call out *"Done!"* over all the noise.

Mr. Santiago looks surprised (or maybe impressed?) when he stops by my table. "Looks . . . good."

Mr. Santiago heads over to his office and returns with a bunch of bananas. "I just so happened to pick these up at the store this morning." He slips them onto the hook. I cross my arms and confidently lean against the table to see my project in action.

I straighten. "Those were too heavy!"

"They're . . . bananas," Jimmy Suarez points out unhelpfully.

"Take your time with projects, Ms. Diaz. I'm sure you'll get it next time."

Even bananas have it out for me.

At home, Abuela spots my failed project before I can toss it. Abuela has a whole list of things we're not allowed to throw away, because they can still be used.

I tell her it's broken, but she just waves my pessimism away and sets it on the counter. She decides it's a great place to dry the sandwich bags she *also* reuses.

In the backyard, I find Dad. The sun's starting to set, but he's got a blueprint spread across the patio table.

"There's my woodworking girl!" Dad says.

He throws an arm around me, then gestures to the

blueprint in front of him. It makes about as much sense to me as pre-algebra.

I tell him about my failed banana holder. "Woodworking is not easy."

"Everything's tough until it isn't," he says. "And then it usually gets tough again. That's life."

Dad saying *That's life* reminds me of Mom telling me that everything is just *temporary*.

They're simple answers that don't feel simple at all.

I study the blueprint and try to imagine it where the bones of Abuela's future tiny house sits. It's under tarps right now to protect it from all the afternoon thunderstorms. A corner of grass will sit between it and our patio. It's kind of hard to picture with everything else going on back here. There's also the grill, all our bikes, and the blow-up pool we have yet to drain and deflate.

"We should make her a garden," I say suddenly, remembering her old one from Homestead.

Dad smiles. "That's a great idea." He scribbles something on the blueprint. "That's out of my wheelhouse. But maybe you could help me with that?"

I know just the club.

I have some experience with farming. Not *actual* farming, but one of my favorite things to build in *BioBuild* is a farm. Collecting seeds from plants, planting everything in neat little rows. It sounds like a chore but is actually really relaxing. But now it's time to take the virtual fun and make it real.

No more fruit stealing for me; it's time to grow my own.

Mrs. Villanueva's biology classroom is near the gym in a sunny corner with lots of windows. There's a side door that leads outside into the bright sunshine. I've already got a great feeling about this club.

"Are you here for the agriculture club meeting?" Mrs. Villanueva asks me.

"I am!" I say happily. "I'm Maggie Diaz."

"Nice to meet you, Maggie," Mrs. Villanueva says. She reminds me a little of our new art teacher, Ms. Pérez, but instead of paint, there's grass stains and dirt on her khaki pants. A butterfly clip holds up her dark hair. The room is empty except for us. I wonder where everyone else is as I go to take a seat.

She blinks, then smiles. "Nope, we'll be meeting outside."

Thanks to a grant from the University of Miami, we have a school garden I had no idea about, but it's full of fruits and vegetables that are used for our lunches. There's even a beehive!

Outside, the agriculture club is already working on the garden.

"All right, everyone, gather 'round." Mrs. Villanueva calls everyone over to the shelf where I notice lots of tools and watering cans. I spy a silver one that I hope I get to use. There are also big scissors. Maybe I'll be able to cut some flowers and bring them home to Mom. Sweeten her up after that disappointing progress report.

Or wait, maybe I'll learn to shape a hedge into a weird design. Like a flamingo. Or a dragon! I can't wait to know what my job will be.

"Happy October, my fellow green-thumbed children of the soil!" Mrs. Villanueva announces.

Mrs. Villanueva must be *really* into gardening.

"We'll be transplanting our eggplant and pepper seedlings today. We'll also be checking the pH of our soil, and then it's time to plant everyone's favorite vegetables! Broccoli and brussels sprouts!"

Big fans of vegetables in this crowd.

Mrs. Villanueva brings out the tiny seedlings. Each one is a small green bud that will somehow grow into an entire vegetable. Even testing the soil is interesting and makes me feel like a budding (ha *ha*!) scientist. Dad would *love* that joke.

As soon as I get home, I tell Mom about my idea of starting our own garden. "It'll be great!" I explain as I drag her away from her pile of textbooks out to the back-yard. "Remember Abuela's flower garden? She'd love it!"

"Your dad already mentioned this, and just like I told him, we don't have a lot of room for a garden. Also, some-one needs to take care of that." Mom points at the tadpoles.

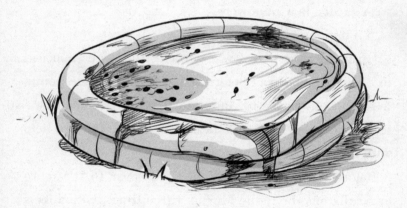

Mom sounds tired and unsure, like she does whenever she's looking for Dad to back her up, but he's on my side about the garden and away at the home improvement store.

"I'll drain the pool," I say, and jump in front of the pool before she notices that some of those tadpoles have morphed into full-on frogs. Mom *hates* frogs. She'll

swat at bugs without flinching, but she's not big on frogs ever since a huge tree frog jumped on her when she was on a ladder.

The whole neighborhood heard her scream.

"And then we'll have room for a garden," I explain.

"A garden is a lot of work."

"I'll handle it," I say.

"First a phone and now a garden? You were supposed to deal with the pool before school started." She points to the spooky house behind ours that's surrounded by a tropical jungle. "Mrs. García has a garden. You can help with hers."

Before I can stop her, Mom walks over to the fence and calls out the name Maruja three times, which feels dangerous and like she's asking for trouble. From between two banana leaves, Mrs. García pops out.

My own mother is no better than Abuela, because

even though Mom isn't asking me to steal an avocado, she volunteers my services without giving me the opportunity to back out.

"There's no gate," I point out as my stomach sinks.

Mrs. García laughs. "We all know you can jump over it, Magdalena."

Mom laughs, too. The avocado thievery is one big joke, and me and my anxiety are the punch line. I bid my mother goodbye, then climb over the fence. I can hear the wind (bone) chimes in the distance as Mrs. García leads me past her roosters and many plants.

She's growing so much stuff out here, but it's nothing like the school garden. There are no wooden beds, or any kind of layout confined by geometry. It's a wild and tangled maze of flowers, vines, and fruits.

For a moment I'm lost, until I spot Mrs. García up ahead and race after her.

"I'm joining the agriculture club at school," I explain as we keep walking. How is her backyard this big? From the other side of the fence, it looks the same size as ours.

When she doesn't say anything, I keep talking. "I asked my mom to start a garden, but she said it's too much work." I glance at the wild space around us and mutter, "You must work out here a *lot*."

She stops suddenly and hands me a small pair of shears. Finally! Dragon hedge, here I come!

"You clip these," Mrs. García orders, pointing at some brown leaves.

"And then what?"

"And then what?" she repeats in a mocking tone. "¡Qué tontería! And *then* I give you more work."

True to her word, Mrs. García takes me all over her garden until the sun starts to set. Every time I start to ask her questions, she quiets me and explains that gardening is about patience.

"I don't think I'm very patient," I tell her.

What else do you want from me?

She ignores me and drops a handful of seeds into my palm and then points me toward an empty spot of dirt. With a fingertip, I push each seed into the soft soil.

"And now what?" I ask.

She grumbles a word in Spanish that I'm not allowed to say and hands me the watering can.

After a while, I don't even mind the quiet. It's kind of nice. Sometimes it feels like I have too many thoughts and they start bumping into each other and turning into worries. Like about how things feel so weird with Zoey now. I wish I hadn't missed her performance. And I wish I had finished the maze in the server. I hate how forgetful I can be sometimes. As soon as I get my laptop back, I'll make the maze and farm so awesome that Julian will forgive me.

I can't mess up with them again.

Mrs. García isn't as scary as I first thought, but I really don't want to make her mad. I still am not totally sure those wind chimes are made of driftwood like Mom said.

When it's nearly dark, I hear Mom's voice call my name.

"I have to go." I'm surprised I feel disappointed.

Mrs. García hands me a bunch of herbs and some peppers. "Mira, dale esto a tu abuela, para que la comida le sepa mejor." She smirks and the light glints off a gold tooth before she waves me off. As I rush through the bushes, leafy vines drag along my arms, making me break out in goose bumps. I keep running toward the small glimmer of porch light. A cat runs past me and I shriek out loud as it hisses.

Back in the safety of my own home, enveloped by the smell of Abuela's soup, I hand her the herbs that are clutched in my hand.

While Abuela goes on about how her food has plenty of flavors, the long day hits me and I fall over on the couch, exhausted. But it's worth it. Because once everything on my plan is checked off, everything will work out. It just has to.

"Did you drain the pool?" Mom asks.

Oops!

☆ CHAPTER 15 ☆

I wake up the next morning to the sound of an electric saw. Dad's working on Abuela's house! I dive off my top bunk to beat Caro to the bathroom before she stinks it up with her hairspray and peach perfume. But when she spots me in the hallway, she freezes. Her eyes get all wide like she's seen a ghost.

"Oh my god, *what* is all over you?"

"Nice try, but you're still too slow," I say, and fly past her.

"You're covered in pimples!"

I scream. From down the hall, Abuela shouts, "¡Señoritas no gritan en esta casa!"

They're not pimples, because they *itch*, and they're *everywhere*.

I run out of the bathroom and Caro actually looks sorry for me when she says, "Yikes."

"Mom!" I wail as I hurry into the kitchen.

Mom looks at me like I've grown two extra heads. "Maggie! *What* did you do?"

Leave it to my mother to automatically assume this is my fault.

"I've been cursed!" I say. "You told me to help Mrs. García and I overwatered her aloe and now she's cursed me!"

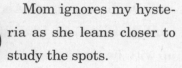

Mom ignores my hysteria as she leans closer to study the spots.

Caro says, "You can't just say people cursed you, Maggie."

Abuela scowls at the window. "¡Lo sabía!" Abuela finishes her examination of my arm and decides, "Pues. Bug bites."

Caro jumps back from me like I'm contagious.

"What?" I shriek, and spin around like they're still on me. I deeply hate most bugs, which is a terrible thing to hate when you live in Florida, because they're literally everywhere. Flying ones, slithering ones, even biting ones. Anytime I walk into a room, I'm on guard to find one.

"You got bit up while gardening." Mom looks over my hands and arms, then yanks my shirt up to check my back. I'm too overwhelmed to be annoyed or embarrassed that I'm in the kitchen in my training bra surrounded by the other women in my family. "And you might be allergic to something you touched."

"Well, don't touch me!" Caro demands, but she's laughing now.

I shake out my arms and whine in distress. "Ugh! I *hate* the outside!" Gardening? Agriculture? What was I thinking?

"Cálmate y ven acá." Abuela calls me over and pops the top on one of her many lotions from her stash in my room. The smell of mint and rotten flowers hits my nose.

Abuela doesn't tell me what's in it before slathering it all over me like sunscreen.

How am I supposed to go to school like this?

Mom and Caro both look concerned, but Mom tries to hide it with a shaky smile. Only Abuela seems unbothered by my appearance.

Caro must feel really bad for me, because she offers to drive me to school.

Caro got her driver's license this year. *Because Caro is a safe driver and a good kid*, Mom likes to remind me whenever I get grumpy about the many things I don't get to do yet even though there are *only* four years between us.

So, *yeah*. Caro is a Very Good Kid who now gets to be a Very Independent Teenager.

The radio station announces the weather (Hot! Like always!) and then introduces that Junior Peña song everyone is listening to.

It is really catchy, but it also makes me sad. I think of Zoey and Julian. I miss how it used to be between us. Before all these new responsibilities and the pressure to figure out who I am.

"It's not that bad," Caro reassures me as I glare out the window. "At least you've been helping Mrs. García out. I'm sure she gets lonely and likes the company."

"It feels like everyone is mad at me," I confess. "And it's hard to figure out where I fit in right now."

Caro laughs and I jerk around in my seat to scowl at her.

She hurries to stop laughing. "I'm not laughing at you, Maggie. But trust me when I tell you I can totally relate."

I roll my eyes. "You're good at everything."

She doesn't even disagree with me.

"I just want to be really good at *one* thing." I'm barely able to keep the whine out of my voice. "Is that so much to ask?" I'm nowhere close to making a skateboard in wood-working, and now I'm covered in bug bites. And I'm not even sure if I like any of the clubs.

"You're good at plenty of stuff," she says.

"Like what?"

When Caro hesitates, I groan.

"Give me a minute," she says quickly. "I am driving, after all. Let's see. You're funny and loyal. Even though you hate it, you're sharing your room with Abuela and moving your stuff around, so she doesn't feel bad. Also, Lucas loves you best."

"I doubt that," I say, though it does make me a little happy to think I could be someone's favorite, even if it is just my slobbery baby brother. "And that's just who I am at home and family stuff. It's not really about me. Like school-version me."

I need something that says Maggie Diaz. Something that's just mine.

"At least Dad will finish Abuela's little house soon." Then everything at home will be back to normal.

Caro laughs. She knows it takes Dad forever to finish stuff.

"Thanks for the ride," I tell her when she pulls up to the front of the drop-off area.

She turns down her radio. "Wait, aren't you going to brush your hair?"

Nice Sister Moment is officially over.

I head toward third hall, but slow down by the band room. The door is open, and the sounds of different instruments warming up spill out of the room. I spot

Zoey, laughing with Maya and others. She's officially been folded into Maya's group. Julian's also spending his mornings in Ms. Pérez's art room with his club. They're working on the mural after school, so he's really busy, too, and always covered in paint.

What if having a phone and getting to hang out at Dolphin Park doesn't actually fix everything?

Yikes.

"Agriculture club," I explain. "Or a bruja's garden. Not sure which, but I'm staying away from plants today."

We settle in to eat our lunches, mostly quiet until I look up and see Julian.

"Hey, stranger!" he says, and my heart almost bursts with relief. He doesn't hate me for messing up our *BioBuild* server! "You sit over here now?" he asks, then glances around me. "Hey, Eddie!"

I scoot closer to Eddie to make room for Julian.

Eddie sighs. "This is going to ruin the quiet."

Julian gives him a friendly grin before digging into his fries. "I'm so happy to be done with testing, let me tell you. Having the later lunch with the eighth graders was killing me." He wolfs down another fry. As he chews, his brows shoot up when he notices the bites. "What happened to you?"

I tell him about agriculture club and Mrs. García's garden. He laughs and most of my worry slips away in one big rush.

"And I thought you were still mad at me," I tell him.

"About *BioBuild*?" He shrugs. "You were busy and grounded. Stuff happens."

"I'm really sorry."

He smiles. "I appreciate that." Julian finishes his lunch. He slips one of his purple markers out of his shirt pocket and asks, "May I?"

I shrug and he grabs my arm and draws a line between my spots.

"What are you doing?" I ask him.

He finishes and then presents my arm back to me. "It's a constellation of Aries. If anyone asks, just call them stars." He grins brightly.

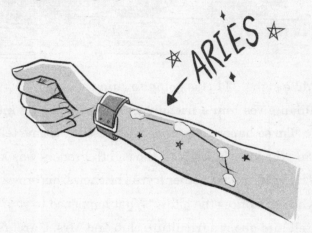

My moodiness is no match against Julian, and I smile back. Even Eddie is impressed. He asks Julian if he's into some artist I've never heard of.

"Oh, yeah!" Julian says. "Did you see his mural in Wynwood?"

Eddie's eyes brighten. I've never seen him so excited. "The goth gator was killer!"

Julian eagerly sits forward and leans over me to tell him all about the mural.

I'm feeling better than I have in a while as I head to math.

"Hey," I say to Zoey.

"Hey," she says. It's quiet for an awkward beat. "So, Julian is done with his testing? I noticed he was back at lunch." I wonder if she misses me, too.

A surge of hope hits me. I can fix this.

That is, until last week's worksheet is returned.

☆ CHAPTER 16 ☆

"Report card day!" Mom announces one early morning. She sounds very chipper. She smiles as she points at the circled date on the calendar. The reminder is printed on today's square like a holiday. This is what I get for giving her the calendar issued to us on the first day of school. "Big day for our Maggie."

"Honor Roll Maggie!" Dad cheers as he serves himself some coffee.

Abuela serves me pan tostado and café con leche in my favorite mug. She squeezes my shoulder proudly.

My confidence has made them certain about this. About me.

Maggie has shown improvement. No tardies this semester and lots of initiative. But Maggie needs to better her math grades.

But now that it's here—*I'm* not so sure anymore.

In homeroom, Mrs. Delgado passes out the yellow envelopes. I *still* have a D in math. No one gets on honor roll with a D. The percentage is closer to a C, but it doesn't matter. It's still a D. I *have* to show this to Mom, thanks to all my bragging and the school calendar.

I hurry out of homeroom. I'm panicking, but there's no way around this. My big plan is a bust. Everything is ruined.

"Hey, are you okay?" Zoey asks me.

I show her my awful report card in reply.

Zoey takes and scans it. She glances up with a happy smile. "Hey, you got social studies and science up from Cs to Bs."

"Who cares about that? Math ruined everything as usual."

"Your whole report card isn't ruined because of one grade, Maggie."

"It will be once my mom sees it," I complain. "She's never going to let me do anything cool, and now everyone is going to keep leaving me behind."

"Who is—" Zoey frowns. "Are you mad at me because I'm in band?"

The bell rings. I want to fix this right now, but I don't know how. Zoey shakes her head and dashes past me to her next class.

By the end of the day, I am a walking stomachache. I don't even get lunch. The fight with Zoey keeps replaying in my head.

But did I really try? The question spins in my head. I'm trying to make a birdhouse in woodworking, but as I hammer in a nail, I get my thumb instead.

I swallow a cry and try to smile for Mr. Santiago.

I *hate* fighting with Zoey. I know it's my fault, but I keep making it worse. I thought it would just be temporary and I could fix it soon. But that's definitely not happening now.

The report card looms from my backpack like a curse.

There is absolutely no way I can spring it on Mom without a plan. That will end up in a *very* bad conversation for me.

Caro picks me up after woodworking, and when we get home, I slip into the house and look for an ally. Dad is hanging out with Lucas in the living room. Some tummy time for my brother while Dad happily reads a book to him.

Dad will be cool about my report card, but he's useless when it comes to running interference with Mom. He'll tell me to just talk to her. *It won't be that bad*, he'll promise me with a big, goofy golden retriever smile, because that's Dad. This situation requires finesse. Calm but smooth self-control. I have to carefully defuse this bomb, or it'll blow up in my face.

Then there's Caro. She knows Mom. She'll understand how careful I have to be with our mother when it comes to presenting stressful information or anything she doesn't want to hear. Mom is always in the middle of doing ten other things at once, and one piece of bad news that upsets her will send our entire house into chaos.

But Caro is also Caro. And I'm pretty sure my big sister would find it very funny for all of this to blow up in my face.

So that leaves me with Abuela. But will she be my ally in this?

I'm so desperate for help and to avoid Mom until I have a real plan, that I offer to go with Abuela to run errands. When we get to the market, I make my move.

"Abuela, I need some advice," I say as I trail after her down the store aisle.

She stops to pick through the green plantains. "¿Sobre qué?"

We stop beside the refrigerated section, and there between the Jupiña and Ironbeer, I slip my report card out of my bag and present it to Abuela.

Abuela glances over it, then hands it back with a blasé shrug. "Está bien, Magdalena."

I shiver from the refrigerated icy cold and nerves. "It's not, though!" Does Abuela even know her own daughter? Missing out on an opportunity with Mom means you have to wait a long time for another shot.

She's kind of like the World Cup in that way.

"Solo necesitas saber cómo hablar con ella," Abuela says as she grabs a bag of rice.

"I know how to talk to Mom, Abuela."

But as I follow her through the store, Abuela reminds me that talking to Mom these days is all about presentation.

When we return home, Dad is giving Lucas a bath, so I take the opportunity of having Mom alone in the kitchen. I silently hand her my report card. She studies it, and before she can say a word, I'm up on my feet, pacing.

"School has gotten harder," I hurry to say, just like I practiced in the car with Abuela on the way home. "And for the first time, I'm busier with extracurriculars."

Mom takes a seat and rubs her temple like she has a headache. She just got home from class. And she still hasn't said a word. A bad sign, because—oh no, *I'm* the headache.

Mom tosses my report card aside. It's all over. She's definitely not putting it on the fridge.

The door opens and Caro walks inside, calling out a hello before pouring herself a glass of water. She's back from one of her runs. She's sweaty and gross, but also smiling.

I'm totally jealous of her. I'm tired of feeling stuck.

An idea hits me, and I look at Mom. "I need more than just academics to get into a good college."

I can almost see the lightbulb pop up over Mom's head. *College.* My mother's kryptonite.

"But I think I need to try something that will add more to my transcripts."

Mom looks confused. "Transcripts? Maggie, you don't have to worry about that right now."

Caro sighs. "Lucky."

I ignore her and focus on Mom. I'm not on honor roll . . . yet, but maybe by showing her how far ahead I'm looking, I can prove how responsible I am now. I'm joining clubs to figure out what I'm into and who I am. I'm working on my grades to earn independence.

"I think it's great that you want to try new things, but I want you to do them because you want to. Because you're interested and curious to learn new things and grow."

It's surprising that Mom's not freaking out. It's a relief and a disappointment. Had she expected this all along?

Caro skips past. Perfect Caro with all the answers. Caro who gets to drive and hang out with her friends.

"I'm going to try out for track," I announce.

CHAPTER 17

Track is just the trick for distracting Mom from my report card and grounding. I put Future Leaders and woodworking on hold in order to save my plummeting grades.

But I still can't believe I picked cross-country of all things. Running is Caro's thing. And the last thing I want is to get myself stuck even more in her shadow.

But there are some pros.

The bad news is that I'm two months too late to sign up for cross-country *and* it's still too early to try out for track. Just another perfect example of my awful timing. But the good news is that being Carolina Diaz's little sister has some benefits. Shocking, I know.

PROS	CONS
☐ I'll get to be outside.	☐ No one will ever forget that I'm Caro's little sister.
☐ I won't technically be just playing.	
☐ I'll be doing a sport.	

When I mention this to Mom, she thinks it will be good for me to have a responsibility that requires me setting my alarm even earlier.

I kind of hate that Caro is older and got to call dibs on running, because once I get up the next morning and head to the track, it's great. I'm outside and I'm moving. I don't have to think about my plans for the future, my disappointing report cards, or how sometimes you mess up so bad with your best friend, they move on to trumpet players.

I'm running instead of worrying that Dad is taking forever to finish Abuela's house and that he'll probably get another job that takes him far away before he finishes. I don't think about how Mom will probably make me wear baby watches forever.

And whether I do have a mustache?

And, and, and, *and* . . .

Coach Schwartz is so impressed with my time, he invites me to their meet this weekend.

After school, I go outside to help Dad work on Abuela's suite. He's using a big circular saw. I'm not allowed anywhere near it, but I help grab stuff for him. Still, though, he makes me wear safety goggles and earplugs.

"I like running," I tell him, pitching my voice louder to continue our conversation. "But it's Caro's thing."

"Who says?"

"Caro and, like, *everyone* else."

Dad pulls the saw down on a piece of wood. It makes a loud, grating sound as it cuts down on the plank, but the earplugs tone the noise down. When he's done, he says, "Why can't running be something you both do? Maybe our family is just really good at running. I mean, not me, but definitely you two."

I take one of Dad's pencils and measure out his next cut. "It feels like everything changed this year. Everyone is in a club or sport. And they're *good* at it. They all have a cool hobby or skill."

"You do lots of stuff, Maggie."

"Maybe," I say. Mom's busy studying for her finals, Caro is spending more time with Alex, and Dad is blasting his emo music in the backyard as he finally finishes Abuela's house. It still feels like I'm just playing around while everyone around me is leveling up.

Speaking of games, Mom has allowed me to have my laptop back. After I finish helping Dad, I race inside to log on to our *BioBuild* server.

magpieOfmischief: guess who's back

magpieOfmischief: it's ah me, maggie

roboJellybean: hey, stranger!!

roboJellybean: did u get ur laptop back?

roboJellybean: or a phone???

magpieOfmischief: uh no phone

magpieOfmischief: just my laptop

roboJellybean: we should send zoey an invite to our server

magpieOfmischief: zoey stopped playing

magpieOfmischief: and hanging out with us

roboJellybean: talk to her!! Communication is key

magpieOfmischief: ok dad

roboJellybean: clean ur room, champ

At school, I try to talk to Zoey. But she's always around other people, and I don't know how to bring it up in the middle of math class. All these extracurriculars and clubs are supposed to help us figure out what we're into, but no one tells you that to figure yourself out, sometimes you have to leave stuff behind.

The next morning at practice, Julian stops in front of me, waving his arms wildly to get my attention.

I slow down. "What's up?"

"Nice form." He gives me a thumbs-up. His fingers are smudged with charcoal. "I just wanted to give you a heads-up that I won't be at lunch."

My stomach starts hurting. My other best friend is about to dump me, too. I want to run away from all these feelings.

Julian waves his arms again even though I'm standing right in front of him. "Whatever you're thinking, *no*, back up."

I take a step back. He smirks.

"It's just a last-minute meeting in the art room about our big mural reveal. It's this Saturday and I really want you to come." He smiles. "Zoey will be there, too, and I really need both of my besties to see it."

I'm reminded of listening to Zoey play her flute all summer and recording herself playing with Maya just so I could hear it. Julian needs me and there's no way I can disappoint him again. And this way I'll get to see Zoey, too.

"I'll be there, I promise!"

CHAPTER 18

My very first cross-country meet is at a nearby high school. It's the last one of the season, so it's especially weird to be the new kid here. It's a big, blue-sky kind of Saturday morning. There's a cool breeze that almost feels like it's finally actually October. Caro is sitting with Alex in the crowd somewhere. She drove me here since Mom has a class and Dad had to go to Port of Miami for work.

I stretch with the other girls around me and try to copy their moves without being obvious. They're mostly eighth graders. They share jokes and stories about past meets. By their excited voices, it doesn't feel competitive.

"I can't believe this is our last meet this year!" one of them calls out once she's done stretching.

"I know! Hopefully our school does a track meet at yours."

"Fingers crossed! I could finally show you around!"

As I listen to their conversations about plans outside of running, I realize they all have friends from different parts of their lives. And it's not a big deal.

We may get busy, but never too busy for you.

Coach Schwartz comes over to talk to us and get us pumped up before the meet starts.

"Now remember to start out quick, get out of the wash, and then into your pace," he says.

"Wash?" I ask. Are we running through water?

Coach Schwartz rubs his eyebrow. He looks like he's regretting letting me attend this meet. Or he's missing Caro.

"Just . . . just run, Maggie," he finally says.

That I can do. I give him a thumbs-up. We get into our positions.

The whistle blows and all the girls around me take off running. I try to get out of the traffic jam of people so I can run at my own pace. At least that part of Coach Schwartz's advice makes sense.

The route we're running takes us past the high school and down along a canal until we reach a nearby park. When I get to the canal, I make sure to stay near the pathway. Rule #1 of Florida: Assume alligators are in any body of water that isn't the beach.

What I really like about running is that I'm able to unscramble my thoughts. As I run, my imagination keeps pace. When I glance at the canal, I remember the water slide I want to build in *BioBuild*. I run past lemon and papaya trees and an ice cream truck, and my thoughts turn to ideas of other fruits and flavors that might make for a good pastelito.

Some runners fly past me, but it doesn't feel like a race.

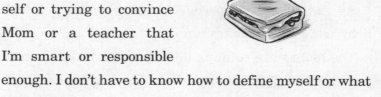

That's their pace and this one is mine.

I'm not comparing myself or trying to convince Mom or a teacher that I'm smart or responsible enough. I don't have to know how to define myself or what I'm good at.

I can just *be*.

Plus, I'm burning off all this energy that I always have. Being alone isn't too bad sometimes. It's nice and quiet.

My heart beats fast.

No baby crying or humming humidifier . . .

No abuela shouting for me to stop shouting . . .

No busy school hallway, new song blasting, noisy off-limits band room . . .

My watch beeps.

Oh . . . *no*. Today is Julian's mural reveal. And I'm going to miss it!

I've already messed up with Zoey and Julian. This is too important!

My friends are important.

I spin in place as I remember Julian telling me the location and Ms. Pérez pointing out the blank wall across from the market and bakery. This park is only a few blocks away from there. I turn around and run against the direction of the other runners.

I race down the sidewalk. And with every step, I know I'm moving farther away from where I'm supposed to be. But I can't think about Mom or how much trouble I'm going to be in right now. Which is *so* much.

I promised Julian I would be there and the *last* thing I want to lose is my friends. Because if I do, what is everything worth without them?

Up ahead, I spot a small group of people standing around the wall. I can't see the wall itself yet, but I really hope I'm not too late.

I can smell the sweet, warm smell of the nearby bakery, but not even Pablo's latest creations can stop me now. (Although I should really mention my idea of a papaya-and-apple pastelito to him.)

Finally, I'm just behind the crowd. I'm about to call out Julian's name when the big sheet behind him falls in a dramatic swoop, revealing his mural.

For the first time, maybe ever, I'm speechless.

It's *amazing*. And bright and cool and *us*. I'm on a mural! Even when Julian was busy creating something great and doing what he loves in art club, he was thinking about us. Maybe I'm not so easily forgotten.

I look over and see Zoey. She's smiling shyly at me. I race over to her.

"I'm so sorry," I tell her in a rush. "I should have said that sooner, but I got so in my head, so of course, I got super confused."

Zoey laughs and it's the best sound ever.

Julian walks over and throws his arms around both of us. "Because communication is key!" he sings out with a big grin.

We head across the street and stop at the window to see Pablo. He's really impressed with the mural and calls Julian a genius. Julian is in total art-geek-out mode as he describes all the ways he used the paint to create dimension and shadows and how cool Ms. Pérez is for picking *his* idea and letting them run with it.

Pablo offers us some croquetas and crackers and even throws in three cans of ice-cold Jupiña.

I tell Pablo about my pastelito idea, and he throws his head back and

laughs until Ms. Pérez walks over to congratulate Julian.

And as we eat, Zoey, Julian, and I have a *conversation* and it's a total relief. My family and friends had the right idea all along. Communicating is *really* important. Especially when stuff starts messing up. You can't to-do list your way out of the tough stuff.

"I just wanted to hurry up and figure out my one true skill," I explain. "Like art and band are for you two. But it felt like I was falling behind in everything, all at once."

"You should have talked to us," Zoey says.

"Communication is—" Julian starts.

"We *know*," Zoey and I interrupt, laughing.

Julian rolls his eyes with an amused smirk.

Zoey elbows me. "Talk to us, even when you don't have all the answers yet."

"*Especially* then," Julian says with a laugh.

Pablo leans against the counter. "As my official taste tester, you know how many tries it takes me to get a dessert right. And I couldn't get there without your help."

Hiding failed tests and progress reports didn't help at all. But being honest about where I messed up and misunderstood does. I've been waiting for everything to fall into place to solve all my problems.

Friends too busy for me? Get busy, too!

No independence? Get a phone and your abuela out of your room!

But waiting for everything to be perfect to fix things doesn't fix anything.

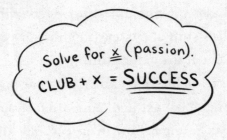

Solve for x (passion).
CLUB + x = SUCCESS

Don't ask me. It turns out seventh grade is pretty complicated and I'm still trying to solve for the unknown.

But I'm glad that I'm able to talk about everything with Julian and Zoey over another plate of croquetas. It reminds me of Mom and how important conversations are in my family. For big stuff, and all the little stuff that can become big if we aren't being honest.

"How was your meet?" Julian asks.

"My what?" I glance down at myself and see my number still pinned to my chest. I gasp. I'm not where my mother thinks I am right now. Again.

She's going to actually *kill* me this time.

"I'm in the middle of the meet!" I cry out.

Zoey and Julian's eyes widen. "Maggie, no!" they both say.

Maggie, yes. I messed up *again*.

"I can't run all the way back!" I say as a familiar car

drives up on the street next to us. It slows down just as the window lowers. The driver slips their big sunglasses down, and Abuela shouts, "¡Apúrate, niña!"

She doesn't need to tell me twice.

I jump into the passenger seat. I'm sweaty and a total mess, but I'm so relieved to see Abuela that I don't even mind her not using the AC.

"Abuela, how did you know where to find me?" I ask, breathless. "Brujería?" She really is a witch!

But Abuela shakes her head. "No, the GPS on your watch." Abuela hits the gas.

When we get home, I see Mom is waiting for us on the porch.

I turn a betrayed look on my supposed ally. "You told her?"

"Your watch did, mi amor," Abuela says gently.

✦ CHAPTER 19 ✦

Mom doesn't say a word. That's how I know I'm doomed. Yelling would've been better. Regular Latina Mom fussing at everyone and the world for not helping her in the exact way she wants to be helped. Typical.

But when she's quiet? Deadly.

Her hair is all gathered in her bun. I have no way to track her anger. But I know there will be no trial this time.

I will be grounded for an eternity.

I start to apologize, but Mom holds up her hand to stop me.

Guilt makes my stomach swim and eyes burn.

"Go to your room, Magdalena."

I trudge past her inside. When I get to my room, it's finally quiet and I'm alone just like I'd wished.

I climb up into my bed, then fall face-first into Teddy the Turtle's shell so no one can see me cry.

Abuela walks in and leans against the bed. With half my face smushed in the pillow, I say, "I just wish she would let me explain."

"Esto no es fácil. She was very worried." Abuela sighs, then tips her head with a soft smile. "Cuéntame qué pasó."

I'm desperate for a chance to explain. I sit up and tell her *everything*.

I tell her about missing my friends all summer. My big plans leading me to trying out all these clubs, but still missing Zoey's performance, and the terrible silence between us. I tell her about Julian's mural reveal and how scared I was that I would disappoint him again, too.

All this work and now I'm grounded. I'm so grounded I'll be lucky to see sunshine before I'm thirteen.

Abuela tries to bring some kind of order to my hair, softly brushing curls behind my ear. The soothing feeling of her fingernails against my scalp reminds me of when I was younger. I used to fall asleep on her lap at family parties. They were always so noisy and busy, but Abuela would bring us extra snacks and a pillow.

The pillow on her lap was a beacon for her sleepy grandbabies to rest while our parents and tías stayed up, gossiping and dancing way past our bedtimes.

She keeps brushing my hair and I finally relax.

For the next couple of weeks, I'm on my very best behavior. I ask for help in math, and Mrs. Bermudez sets me up with the high school's tutoring club. Instead of packing my schedule with clubs, I'm now getting help from Alex on Monday and Wednesday afternoons.

By November, the D in math is a very nice C. Mrs. Bermudez congratulates me, and I'm optimistic that I can get it to a B before my next report card. Slow but steady.

When I get home, I drop the graded quiz on the table in front of Mom and then dash to my room. Maybe if I stay out of her immediate eyeline, she'll eventually forget all about the meet.

Caro stops in my room after dinner, and I'm bored enough to ask what she wants. Since I'm grounded, I can't even play on my Switch or the laptop.

"What is it?"

"You want to go on a run with me?" she asks.

I finally look over and notice she's in her running clothes. The cross-country season is over for her, too. I wish I'd had more time.

"With you?"

She rolls her eyes. "No, with the ice cream man. Come on."

Caro takes off down the sidewalk and I hurry to catch up. As we start to run through our neighborhood, I can't help but cut quick looks at Caro beside me. Is this a race? Should I try to be faster than her?

But after we turn the corner at the next block, I realize we're keeping pace. And it's nice.

Maybe running *can* be something we both do. Because *maybe* it isn't totally terrible to be a little bit like my sister.

When we reach our street again, I spot Mrs. García in her front yard, watering her rosemary. I slow to wave at her.

And Caro speeds up.

"Hey!" I take off to race after her.

She reaches the driveway first and jumps in a celebratory cheer. "Always save your sprint for the end," she boasts.

I huff and puff, trying to catch my breath. But I smile. Because now I know for next time. She's so toast.

The sound of the drill leads me to the backyard and inside the suite.

The progress on Abuela's tiny house is way further along now. It's not just a wooden frame anymore. There are actual

walls. Even the bathroom is almost finished and just needs a curtain for the tub and all those pink fluffy tissue box holders and accessories Abuela likes.

"Looks pretty good in here, huh?" Dad asks. A tool belt is slung on his hips. He turns in a circle.

"It really does," I say. "I had no idea you already did all of this."

He laughs. "I'm slow but steady. It's how I work best."

One thing I've learned from running is that we all have our own pace.

"She'll be out of your room in no time," Dad assures me.

To my surprise, I don't feel very happy about the news.

Dad hands me a mallet. "Want to help me get down the rest of this laminate flooring?"

Laying down flooring isn't as exciting as making a skateboard, but there is something satisfying about seeing the pieces click together in place. After an hour and a

half of Dad's screamo playlist, Abuela's bedroom floor is finished.

She's going to be out of my room so soon.

"Look at us," he says. "Dad and Daughter Flooring. We would totally rock at that."

"I think I'm going to be a one-hit wonder." I return his mallet.

"That's fair. Go out while you're on top." He raises his hand for a high five. "At least you can say you tried it."

I've been trying a lot of stuff lately.

Before returning inside to the mind-numbing silence of my electronic-less punishment, I head to the fence. As I get closer, I can hear the spooky chimes. I poke my head past the banana leaves and spot the roosters. But no Mrs. García.

"Ven acá," she orders, and my heart is still racing, but I jump over the fence and follow her into the jungle of her backyard. Now that Mrs. García has taken a shine to me

and I'm *pretty* sure her roosters won't attack me, I love how different it feels back here. It's like a hidden oasis where I can hide away from all the noise for a little while. Once I'm past the banana leaves, I can't hear Dad's tools or any of our other neighbors.

I expect Mrs. García to give me a task, but instead, she points to the small flower-  pot where she let me plant seeds a couple of weeks ago.

Mrs. García gives me an *I told you so* look.

Patience, she'd told me.

She leaves me alone with the baby plants, and I care- fully water them.

CHAPTER 20

Winter break starts next week, and Mom is letting me play *BioBuild* again. I've finished up the maze and zombie pig farm, and also built a working Ferris wheel. Julian is thrilled. And since I'm not allowed to hang out after school (RIP Dolphin Park and the phone I never got), Zoey has started to play *BioBuild* with us again.

magpieOfmischief: wow cool username zoey

Zo5689756: I couldn't log into my old acct!!

roboJellybean: that's a lot of numbers

Zo5689756: my mom would kill me if I use my real name online

magpieOfmischief: fair

roboJellybean: can yall pls come check out this water slide

roboJellybean: I finally get to show this place off

Zo5689756: this is actually pretty cool

Zo5689756: wow that rollercoaster is huge

magpieOfmischief: if only we could hang out somewhere like this for real

Zo5689756: just talk to your mom

roboJellybean: communication is key

roboJellybean: also pls go to the waterslide!!

magpieOfmischief: talking to her will never work

Zo5689756: what have we learned this year? Hmmmmm??

Zo5689756: JULIAN

Zo5689756: the waterslide dumps you into lava!!!

roboJellybean: AHAHAHAHAH

roboJellybean: it's a carnival of DOOM

At school, all the club flyers have mostly disappeared. I guess there will be new ones after break.

I still don't know if I've "found" myself or what my obvious super skill is. But I did learn some new things about myself. I really like volunteering. It can be so rewarding. I've also learned that I need to be more mindful of the environment and to never litter when I go to the beach. The ocean and sea turtles deserve better.

Also, never judge a boy by his goth nickname.

I also learned that woodworking is pretty awesome. And dangerous. But mostly awesome. I plan to sign back up again once I'm done with tutoring. I want to see what kind of stuff they get to build in eighth grade.

Gardening was also fun, but it requires a lot of patience. And it can sometimes be even more dangerous than woodworking.

SCRATCH
SCRATCH
SCRATCH

But most of all, I've learned that I *really* like running. I want to get faster and for my legs to get all muscly. I want to learn to run so fast I become unstoppable. I want to go to meets on the weekends and run into friends from other schools and laugh about last year's meet like, *Hey, remember when we saw that alligator?*

Which is why I plan on trying out for the track-and-field team in the spring. I don't know if I'll like track as much as cross-country, but there's no way to know unless I try.

I head to PE and meet up with Zoey and Julian. After changing into our gym clothes, Zoey and I meet Julian outside the locker room. "Disc golf, battle ball, or relay races?" he asks us. It's Fun Friday before winter break. All around the soccer and track field they've set up fun activities, and we get to choose whatever game we want to play.

My arm shoots up for the relay races.

Zoey laughs. "You are such an athlete now."

As we walk toward the races, I tell them my worries that I won't like track and field as much as I did cross-country.

"There are songs I don't like to play for band," Zoey says. "But I still love playing my flute."

Julian nods. "And there's plenty of stuff I don't like to draw, but it helps me get better."

Clubs really can be different. The chance to choose for myself and get better at something I like is exciting.

When Coach Schwartz blows the whistle, Julian runs the first part. I scream my head off along with everyone else around us. When he hands the baton to Zoey, I stop screaming, because I know I'm next.

My heart jumps like it did at the meet. I *love* this feeling. It's chaotic and thrilling. But the other team's runner is just ahead of Zoey.

I *run*.

This is different than setting my pace for cross-country practice. This is like a shaken soda can being opened. Like Dad turning his screaming emo music all the way up in the car. This is my best friends shouting my name for us to win.

The other team beats us by a hair. But we all laugh and high-five. Turns out sprinting is also *awesome*.

I don't *have* to try everything, but I should definitely try whatever I like before I talk myself out of it. And one day, I'm going to build that skateboard I've always dreamed of. Because, breaking news: I don't have to like just *one* thing.

After school, on my way to my bike, I spot Mrs. Villanueva by the school garden. I head over to say hi and check on the peppers and eggplants.

I tell her about the seedlings I started in Mrs. García's wild jungle garden, and Mrs. Villanueva practically throws a parade over the news. She tells me that I'm definitely a fellow green thumb. Maybe I'll start with gardening and work my way up to neighborhood bruja. I can't wait to see the seedlings grow into peppers that I'll dare Julian to eat.

"Don't be a stranger, Maggie," Mrs. Villanueva tells me. "Even if you aren't in agriculture club, this garden is yours, too."

When I get home, I go straight to my room. The only path out of my eternal punishment is to get my grades back up. Maybe not to straight A's or even honor roll. If I keep improving, I know that will go a long way to impressing Mom.

But when I get to my room, I crash to a stop. My backpack falls off me like a bag of rocks.

I run outside to the backyard. There's a tiny mint-green house with white trim and a blue door. There's a redbrick pathway between her door and the back porch, and a brand-new flower garden. Abuela's new tiny house is actually real.

"We're not roommates anymore." It comes out like I'm whining. My room's mine again. I don't have to listen to her humidifier or worry about stolen batteries. I can go back to my bottom bunk. It won't smell like mint and old-lady perfume anymore.

Why is my throat feeling tight?

Abuela gives me a tour, and it's so great to see her in her own space.

I realize that as much as I've wanted my independence, so has Abuela.

✵ CHAPTER 21 ✵

After school, I find Mom in the living room. Dancing.

There are several reasons why my mom might be dancing:

But also, because she's stressed, and she has to dance the nervous energy out. Kind of like me with running.

I check the calendar. Mom's last final is tomorrow, and so this is definitely stress dancing. I call it the Distraction Mambo.

"Mom!" I break her flow and hand over my progress report. She reads it. The seconds feel like minutes as the song changes.

"Looking good, Maggie," she says, and hands it back. Lucas shrieks and she bends to pick him up out of his nearby Pack 'n Play.

Her tone is good but not great. Not *fireworks in the sky over Biscayne Bay* wow. I wish I could give her straight A's just once, but that's starting to feel impossible.

"It's not honor roll," I say, disappointed. "But I'm going to try and get there for my next report card."

Mom looks at me for a long moment. "You know what's my favorite part?" She taps the comment about my improvement. So it is impressive!

"It's not enough to get me out of trouble, though."

"I don't like it when you're not where you say you're going to be. But I have to trust you."

I look down, feeling really bad.

"And I'm so proud of all this energy you've put into

figuring out who you are this year. It's hard to reinvent ourselves. Trust me. I know."

"And all this new independence does scare me. You're going to be thirteen soon." She says this like I'm a hurricane on the horizon and we're all doomed. Maybe my new nickname should be Hurricane Maggie?

"I'll still be the same person." I shrug.

"I know," she agrees with a heavy sigh.

I know changes are coming. I also know that I can't wait for everything to be perfect in order to be happy. I'll just end up missing out on lots of stuff.

Caro walks into the kitchen. And she's got Alex with her.

Mom and Alex greet each other with a quick

hug. Caro looks nervous. Alex says hi to me like we're old friends. I update her on my latest math grade, then ask her about her surfboard.

"It's awesome!" she says. "You should come out to the beach with us sometime."

Surfer Maggie? Why not!

Mom's radio does a quick advertisement in rapid-fire Spanish before introducing the Junior Peña song *everyone* is listening to.

Mom's eyes brighten. "I love this song!" Just before I can stop her, she grabs my hand and pulls me into a dance. It's her happy *I love you and you're totally my favorite kid* dance, so I follow along.

On the morning of Mom's graduation, the house is in chaos. As usual.

Abuela is the first one to wake up. By the time I get up, she's already dressed, her hair curled and smelling strongly of powdery perfume. Abuela congratulates me for being the next person awake. It's *totally* a contest for her.

In the kitchen, Lucas drums against the table of his high chair, demanding attention. Or croquetas. I sleepily distract him with silly faces that delight him while Abuela makes me pan tostado and a mug of café con leche.

Mom flies out of her room in her graduation gown, but no pants. She reports that Dad's nose is stuffy and tears through the kitchen 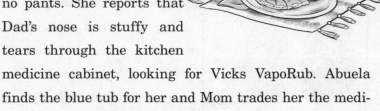 medicine cabinet, looking for Vicks VapoRub. Abuela finds the blue tub for her and Mom trades her the medicine for her pants, begging Abuela to iron them.

I know what Mom needs to calm down. I take out my phone.

Yes, you heard me!

Maggie Diaz has a phone!

I scroll over to my freshly downloaded music app and play some bachata for Mom. She slows her pacing as she finds the rhythm to the song. Dad trudges into the room, looking and sounding very sleepy and sniffly. Mom tugs him into the dance with her anyway. His eyes are barely open, but he smiles and skillfully slips right into the song with her.

I hold my phone up and record them.

maggie of mischief Apr 14
CONGRATS MOMMY 🎓 #dancechallenge
#bachata #sillyparents #collegegraduation

Not to post it anywhere to go viral (no social media until thirteen) but just to keep as a memory.

After Mom's graduation, everyone's gathered in the backyard to celebrate, but I grab my bike because it's *finally* time. My big moment is here.

"See you later!" I call out.

Dad's grilling pork that Abuela marinated for hours, so I'll definitely be back before dinner. Caro and Alex are kicking a soccer ball around. Dad lifts his hand for a high five as I pass him. Abuela waves from her chair in front of her tiny house, Lucas in her lap.

"Be safe!" Mom calls after me.

She's a happy brand-new college graduate. And I'm a girl with a bike, phone, and my parents' permission to ride *all* the way to Dolphin Park, where my two best friends are waiting for me.

Maya and Eddie are going to meet us there later. I plan to rope them all into planning our own Beach Cleanup.

I ride down the sidewalk, and when I pass the school, my stomach dips down to my toes when I cross the boundary. Even though I'm allowed and Mom knows exactly where I am and where I'm going.

My new phone buzzes. Worrying that it's Mom, I quickly stop to check it.

You found my salt line!

I knew it! She *is* a bruja!

I keep riding and pass the bakery and Julian's mural.

I finally get to Dolphin Park and meet Zoey and Julian by the picnic table. I drop my bike next to theirs.

"I have big news," I tell them.

"You got your room back?" Julian asks.

"Yup," I happily announce. "But that's not it."

"You got your grades up?" Zoey wonders.

"I did! But that's not it, either," I say, and then hold up my phone.

"No way!" Julian shouts.

Zoey cheers, then they both immediately smother me in a hug.

I finally rode my bike to Dolphin Park! And my mom not only knows where I am, but she trusts me enough to be right next to the ocean, unsupervised and with my friends.

I'm out of the baby crib and running through life at my own pace. And while I don't have unlimited data yet, I know I just need time and my next big plan.

SNAP!

Acknowledgments

This book has been such a welcome trip home, and it brought me so much joy in the midst of a really hard year. Maggie was my pandemic support buddy, both of us stuck at home, so hungry to get out of the house and see our friends. Her story is about community, and community is how this story came about, honestly. All the abrazos and gratitude to my sharp, brilliant, fellow 305-till-I-die editor and friend, Shelly Romero. Bonding over the rites of passage that come with growing up moody, angsty Latinas listening to emo music in a tropical climate has meant so much to me and Maggie's story. Thank you for believing in me whenever I worried whether this YA author could write a MG story.

A huge Team Maggie thank-you to the incredible Courtney Lovett. Your amazing art brought these characters, setting, and story to life in a way that has blown me away every step of the way. And to Maeve Norton for being as creative and cool as Ms. Pérez. Thank you for taking my words and Courtney's art and designing this bright, beautiful book. Thank you to Lizette Serrano and Emily Heddleson for inviting me to present Maggie's story to the whole team and giving me a chance to talk about my middle school existential crisis over verbs, independence, and swiping those avocados. Thank you to Sarah Herbik and Sydney Niegos for showing this story so much love and Melissa Schirmer for keeping this project running smoothly. I'm very grateful to everyone at Scholastic who has embraced this story and made me feel so welcome. It is a total dream to be published by you.

I am forever thankful for my agent, Laura Crockett. You're right there through every plot twist, always so confident in my ability to tell my story. Thank you to Brent, Uwe, and Team Triada for helping us navigate every step of this wild publishing journey.

To my mama, who has shown me the power and grace that comes with reinventing ourselves as our dreams and lives change. Thank you for never *really* leaving me when you told me to hurry up and grab that neighbor's fallen avocado. Thank you to my big sister for all those bass-heavy rides to school and my first hoop earrings. And to my baby brother, who may be taller than me nowadays, but I bet you still think I'm pretty cool. (Yeah . . . probably not.) To my dad, who I miss so much. Part of me will forever be that kid waiting for you to come home, but I'm so grateful for every memory and story you gave us, like perfect, hilarious souvenirs.

To my kids: Your school years were turned upside

down, but I watched both of you adapt, grow, and roll with every single change. Here's to all of our *Minecraft* worlds, *Stardew* farms, and perfectly lazy days. And to Craig for making me laugh even when I get all angsty because life feels stressful, small, or overwhelming. I love you three for making anywhere feel like home.

And to you, reader: I hope you take all the time you need to figure out who you are. Seventh grade and all the years after are a pretty great time to find yourself again and again and again.